LT
M
BARNARD

S0-AWC-994

A Hovering of
Vultures

A Hovering of Vultures

Robert Barnard

Thorndike Press • Thorndike, Maine

Published in 1994 by arrangement with Charles Scribner's Sons, An Imprint of Macmillan Publishing Company.

Thorndike Large Print ® Cloak & Dagger Series.

The tree indicium is a trademark of Thorndike Press.

The text of this Large Print edition is unabridged.
Other aspects of the book may vary from the original edition.

Set in 16 pt. News Plantin.

Printed in the United States on acid-free, high opacity paper. ∞

Library of Congress Cataloging in Publication Data

Barnard, Robert.
    A hovering of vultures / Robert Barnard.
      p.   cm.
    ISBN 0-7862-0141-X (alk. paper : lg. print)
    1. English literature — Societies, etc. — Fiction.
    2. Yorkshire (England) — Fiction. 3. Large type books.
    I. Title.
    [PR6052.A665H68   1994]
    823'.914—dc20   93-42056

IN MEMORY OF CHRIS
COMRADE (UP) IN ARMS

Chapter 1

Setting the Scene

Mrs Marsden set out the enamel saucepans on the griddle in front of the open fireplace, alongside the blackened kettle. Tomorrow, maybe, she would put carrots and turnips in them, and perhaps lay a couple of pork chops on the griddle itself. The idea of having a real fire in the grate had been ruled out. Too dangerous, with so many people. On the table nearby was a chipped earthenware bowl, with a floury rolling-pin beside it. Everything had to be that bit higgledy-piggledy, even dirty, Mr Suzman had said. To present a sanitised, pretty-pretty farmhouse kitchen would go against all the visitors' idea of Susannah Sneddon and her novels.

Not that it was a kitchen as such, merely one end of the large ground floor of the farmhouse. Standing back to survey her preparations Mrs Marsden could see into the area

7

that the Sneddons had used as their living space, occupying two-thirds of that floor: here there were old easy chairs, a heavy sofa with its stuffing exposed in places, and desks under both the windows. The desk that Susannah had (perhaps) used was laden with brownish typescript and books, and in the centre was a heavy old typewriter. The desk that Mr Suzman said that Joshua had certainly used had bills and chits, a large account book, and a smaller pile of unused old typing paper. On hooks inside the door hung heavy farming coats, slippers were by the fire, and the oil lamp in the centre of the dining table had a very old box of Bryant and May beside it.

Of course the headquarters of the new Sneddon Fellowship wasn't authentic, wasn't "real" — Mrs Marsden knew that better than anybody. A farmhouse — especially a poor farmhouse — in her childhood days was much dirtier and much smellier than this was allowed to be. In fact the most authentic thing about it was probably the smell that drifted in through the window when it was opened, and this was a mere shadow of the smells that had pervaded farmhouses in her childhood. She walked towards the window that overlooked the farm itself. Now *that* was just as it had been in Susannah's time: the bleak, windswept landscape looking out over the West Yorkshire hills towards Lancashire. The fields and hedges were only now beginning to lose some of their threatening bareness with the late coming of Spring, and on the brow of the hill the bleak little spinney looked bony and ominous, with no sign of new leaves. This was the very view that Susannah had looked out on when writing *The Barren Fields*.

Mrs Marsden busied herself round the living room, and then went upstairs to check on the bedrooms. She valued her job, which had come to her unexpectedly and almost accidentally: she was one of the few people still living in Micklewike who had had a farm upbringing in the area in the 'thirties; thus she could act not only as cleaner and custodian of the farmhouse, but adviser to the Fellowship as well. She was also one of the few people around who still had memories of Susannah and Joshua, though to be sure her memories were hazy, for the Sneddons had hardly been thought anything special in the village at the time. Quite the reverse, in fact. An incompetent farmer and his dreamy slatternly sister. But the fact of her having these memories would no doubt be discreetly bruited about. And Mrs Marsden took pleasure in her mild celebrity and in her new job. It suited her down to the ground. For much of the year it would be occasional and part-time: if a visitor turned up, a notice on the farmhouse door would direct him or her to Mrs Marsden's cottage. During the coming weekend, though, and for a few days after that it would be very much full-time, as it would be for the two months of the schools' summer holidays: many of the Sneddons' new admirers were young people.

And many were old people too, people older than herself who had been readers of Susannah Sneddon's books back at the time when they were first published. She thought this as she ran an unnecessary cloth around the lavatory seat in the unhistorical smallest room, installed by later owners of the farm in the late 'forties. Unhistorical it might be, but a godsend it was, for herself now and for countless visitors in the future. The old had uncertain control of their bladders and bowels. They could not be expected to trot down to the village every time they felt a call of nature.

The sound of a car pulling up at the gate sent Mrs Marsden down the rickety (but discreetly strengthened) stairs. That would be Mr Suzman. Sometimes when he came over from his holiday cottage in Oxenthorpe he liked to leave his car in the little Mickle-wike car park and potter through the village: past the poky general stores where Susannah Sneddon had shopped, past the Black Horse, where Branwell Brontë had drunk (as where had he not?) and where even Joshua Sneddon had enjoyed a quiet pint when he was in funds. But today was a busy one, the last before the hordes descended, and he had left his car (as he insisted visitors would *never* be allowed to do, though special arrangements were to be made for the disabled) down by the gate, on the verge of the road to the village.

Mr Gerald Suzman was portly, but he walked the path from the road with a sprightliness that belied his considerable expanse of belly. He had a grey goatee beard and a sharp eye, and if he occasionally rubbed his hands together it was as an expression of pleasure or satisfaction, not a Heep-like tic to ingratiate himself. Mr Suzman had no need to ingratiate himself: he was a figure of some note in the world of letters.

He rubbed his hands now, as he stood in the doorway and surveyed the interior of High Maddox Farm.

"All ready, eh, Mrs Marsden?"

Gerald Suzman got on well with Mrs Marsden, and was sure that in her he had

11

found a treasure. She was quick and knowledgeable, and she not only anticipated his wishes, but contributed intelligently herself.

"I think so, sir, as far as can be. Of course it's all too clean, to my way of thinking, too much of a museum . . ."

Gerald Suzman sighed.

"Still? That was the feeling I was trying to avoid. But I suppose it's inevitable. Short of dirtying it artificially, what could we do? The visitors will tramp in dirt, of course."

"But it won't be farm dirt. Happen there's nothing we can do about that. At least this weekend we won't have a turnstile."

"Turnstile? We shall never have a turnstile!" He chuckled momentarily. "Do you know Salisbury Cathedral has a turnstile? A turnstile where the visitor is supposed to make a *voluntary* contribution. There's no hypocrisy like religious hypocrisy, is there? I don't know a cathedral from which all sense of spiritual things has fled more completely. No, no: a turnstile would totally ruin the atmosphere of High Maddox."

"What shall we have, then?"

"I'll put a discreet table by the door, with a small cash box."

"That's difficult, if I also show them round," said Mrs Marsden. "People will snitch anything these days."

"A chain, perhaps? And during the summer months a student, just to take the money? We'll think of something. By the summer I expect to have made several distinct improvements. I hope that we'll have *all* the first editions, including Joshua's, and I'll have all the original dust-jackets framed on the wall. There'll be some more typescripts too, and other little things . . ."

"I could never understand why Mr Joshua's books are so valuable," said Mrs Marsden, thoughtfully. "When everybody says they're such poor stuff."

"Rarity value," said Gerald Suzman briskly. "Nobody bought them at the time. Ten years ago you might have picked one up in a second-hand bookshop for 5p. Now, with the interest in the Sneddons so high — " He spread out his hands, as if the sky was the limit. "And at High Maddox we don't admit that they're poor."

"Just different, sir. I know."

"By the way, Mr Randolph Sneddon will be arriving today."

"Oh yes, the — grand-nephew, is it?"

"No, something remote in the cousin line."

"Oh yes, of course. There were no brothers and sisters, were there? I've not had the pleasure of meeting the gentleman."

"No doubt you will tomorrow. I think we

13

should make him an Honorary Vice-President of the Fellowship, when it is set up. Or perhaps a Council member. He has no particular knowledge of Susannah and Joshua, or of their works — no reason why he should: they died before he was born. But he *is* a link."

"Of course, sir. Will he be staying at the Black Horse?"

"No, no. Not really comfortable enough for him. Young Randolph is something rather hectic in the City. He'll be staying at the Duke of Cumberland, in Batley Bridge, and I fear he'll find even that a trifle rough and countrified."

"We don't go in for four-star hotels around here," said Mrs Marsden defensively. "It's not that that folk come for."

"You're quite right. And I'm sure he'll understand that. His father was from Abbotsford, after all, originally — not three miles away. I'm expecting him to help entertain the visitors, and perhaps talk to reporters. We have several members of the press coming . . . It will be a busy two days for you, Mrs Marsden."

"Nothing I like more than a bit of busyness, sir. Now and then, of course. I'll be happy to put my feet up come Monday."

"Perhaps we should go around the house

just once more, and go over what you are going to say to the visitors. After all, we have to remember that these people are not just casual trippers. These are fans — and knowledgeable ones. Founder members of the Sneddon Fellowship. We owe it to them to get it right."

So they went through the farmhouse room by room, going over yet again the pieces of furniture that were authentic and the pieces that were merely of the kind seen in farmhouses at that period. Mr Suzman pointed out that some of the manuscript pages on the desk were the original typescripts, and he drew attention through the windows to features of the landscape that were recognisably used in one or other of Susannah's novels. This final rehearsal was a mere going through of a routine already well tried. There was no question Mrs Marsden knew her stuff — had known it for weeks. When the two of them landed up at last in the kitchen area she said:

"And how many are you expecting, sir, over the weekend?"

"Call me Gerald, please, I wish you could. My calculation is seventy or eighty, at the very least. Plus a lot of mere trippers."

"Gracious heaven! Where will they all be accommodated?"

"Many are native Yorkshire people and Lancastrians. They'll go home in the evenings. There's still plenty of slack at Haworth at this time of year — lots will go to bed and breakfast places there. And there's Batley Bridge, Halifax — I know of one family that has ended up staying in Colne. None of these places is far, as you know, and many of the visitors will have cars. Probably there are some with caravans and tents."

"I'm a bit worried about this place. It's going to be very crowded, isn't it?"

"I'm afraid so, especially just before and just after the meetings. We may have to restrict access at times. Perhaps have a series of viewings every half hour. Yes — that's the best idea."

"I was just thinking, sir, if I'm showing folks around upstairs, there's no one keeping an eye on things down here. I know some of the papers are just copies, but there are the Susannah Sneddon typescripts, and those first editions you say are so valuable . . ."

"I shall be here, and I shall do my bit of escorting round. If you are upstairs I shall be downstairs. Not that I think you need worry. These are fans, and very respectable people. Still, I hope they'll be a lively, varied bunch: plenty of young people, people from all walks of life. We don't want to be too respectable. There used to be an air of smug, middle-class self-congratulation about the Brontë Society, and I wouldn't want the Sneddon Fellowship to get like that. Though the Brontë people have livened up an awful lot recently."

"I wouldn't know about that, sir."

"No, no, of course not."

"Oh, one more thing, sir."

"Yes?"

Mrs Marsden was showing signs of hesitation. Eventually she just pointed towards the floor by the kitchen grate.

"Do I say anything about that, sir?"

He was always telling her to call him Gerald, but she could never quite manage it. He fingered his little beard.

"Ah yes, that is the question, isn't it? On the whole I think *not*. With the more casual trippers you will get in the summer I think yes — it's regrettable, but that's the sort of thing they will be looking for. With most of our visitors this weekend, I feel they would appreciate a more tasteful approach, a more discreet one. So I would say if they ask, then point it out and move straight on. Otherwise don't mention it."

Mrs Marsden nodded her agreement, but

17

the two of them lingered for a moment, still looking down at the brown stain on the bare floorboard, stale witness to the fact that it was there, close by the kitchen range, that Joshua Sneddon had killed his sister with an axe, before going out into the spinney at the end of the field and shooting himself.

Chapter 2

The Actors Assemble

The InterCity 125 pulled out from Kings Cross on time and began its leisurely journey to Leeds. As usual it was full-ish, though there were a few empty seats left for passengers getting on at its usual stopping places. Some of the travellers were still fussing with baggage and getting down books and reading glasses for the journey; others were wondering when the buffet-bar would open. Gregory Waite heaved his rucksack and his girl-friend's neat little suitcase on to the rack and sat down, grinning at her.

"You're a smart packer, I'll give you that," he said. "That suitcase is as light as air."

"I was just thinking it odd that you should need so much more for a walking holiday than I need for a cultural one," said Gillian Parkin, shaking her lustrous bobbed brown head of hair.

"No mystery about that. I'll be roughing it while you're in the lap of luxury at the Black Horse."

"From what I hear of it the Black Horse is far from the lap of luxury. It's a rather dingy pub these days, in spite of its associations with Branwell Brontë and Joshua Sneddon."

"Did Joshua drink, in the serious sense?"

"No, that wasn't one of his problems."

"What was? You'd better tell me the essential points about this pair, so that I can at least hold my own tonight."

Gillian Parkin sighed. She was an intelligent, enthusiastic twenty-four year old, and it always depressed her when people hadn't heard of her thesis topic.

"You really ought to know about them," she said. "It's not as though you don't read."

"I read plenty. I'm a very well-read oik. I just haven't caught up with Susannah and Joshua Sneddon. If anyone had asked me out of the blue I suppose I'd have guessed they were characters from a minor Thomas Hardy novel."

"Well, they're not. They were brother and sister, born on this rather bleak farm just outside Micklewike. Their mother was very religious, but also a great reader — dreamy, romantic. She saw education as a means of escaping from a life she hated, or at least as a means of escape for her children. This meant the children always had books about them — they used to trudge down to the free library at Batley Bridge at least once a week."

"When was this? Victoria's last years?"

"Edwardian, more like. Though they were both born in the early 'nineties. Joshua joined up in 1914, but he was invalided out quite soon. And he had to take over the farm when his father died in 1916, though there is abundant evidence that it's the last thing he would have done by choice. Their mother died in the great influenza epidemic just after the Armistice, and from then on they were there on their own."

"Scribble, scribble, scribbling?"

"Yes, pretty much so. It's thought they wrote a lot in childhood, but none of it survives beyond the odd school exercise book. But Susannah's first book was accepted and published in 1921."

"Hot breathing in the hedgerow?"

Gillian looked at him disapprovingly.

"Be your age. It was rural, yes, and there was love interest, yes. I've never seen why the combination of those two things should be regarded as funny."

"Sorry I spoke. Go on."

21

"Well, from then on there was a book every year or eighteen months until she died. There was a mild success with *Between the Furrows* in 1923, and something of a succès-de-scandale with *The Barren Fields* in 1927. The Home Secretary, Joynson-Hicks, wanted to ban it."

"Is that the man Waugh was getting at? 'Powerful against literature, the Home Secretary'?"

"You are a *very* well-read oik."

"You are too kind, lady . . . Anyway, no prizes for guessing what they were getting up to in the barren fields, or even between the furrows. How did she summon up all this steamy passion? Who was the man in her own life? Not her brother, I hope?"

"Well, there is a school of thought that says so, but not a large one. There are suggestions that she was in love with a farmer from over Oxenthorpe way."

"What happened? Killed in the trenches?"

"He was married. There were difficulties, in those days, if one of you happened to be married."

This was a thoroughly underhand reference to an episode in Gregory's past to which he himself had confessed, in an unguarded moment. He ignored it.

"What about the brother? He wrote too, didn't he?"

"Yes — most unlikely books. He was bitten by the modernist bug — read early Joyce, Ezra Pound, all that sort of thing. He wrote experimental novels published by a tiny publishing firm called the Frolic Press. Perhaps this name led the critics to assume the books were just meant as a joke, though the humour was often very bitter. Anyway, they met with nothing but ridicule, when they were noticed at all. They sold in tens, and Joshua made practically no money from them. The farm was often in difficulties because he was a lousy farmer."

"Walking around thinking of agenbite of inwit when he should have been ploughing a straight furrow?"

"Something like that."

"Meanwhile the sister was doing rather well? So what was the relationship between them like?"

"More and more fraught, apparently. They only had each other, you see. Neither of them mixed much in the village."

"By the way, how do you *know* the situation between them got more and more fraught?"

"By the result."

"Unscholarly, but go on."

"When Susannah had free time she wrote. Joshua had very little, but he did manage three slim novels. Tension grew and grew. Even the village must have sensed it, because there was very little surprise when it happened."

"When what happened?"

"One day in 1932 Joshua got a brief note from the Frolic Press rejecting his fourth book. He brooded over it all morning. Then he came into the kitchen with an axe and killed Susannah. He made himself a cup of tea, wrote a note that just said 'I did it', then went out into the little wood nearby and shot himself through the head. Like everything else he did, his suicide was not a great success. He was still alive when they found him, though he died on the way to the hospital."

"My God, what a story!" said Gregory Waite appreciatively. "It sounds like *Wuthering Heights* rewritten by Joe Orton. It must have knocked the tabloids for six at the time."

"They didn't have tabloids — or not many — at the time. Actually there wasn't all that much publicity. Micklewike was pretty remote then — it wasn't a touristy area, as it is now — and Susannah just wasn't well-known *enough* for the newspapers to get

24

hysterical. There was a very mild sensation, which probably led to one or two reprints of the early novels. That was about it."

"Until when?"

"Until the Untamed Shrew Press came along, early in the 'eighties, and reprinted *The Barren Fields* and then all the others. Since then interest has grown and grown."

"Among whom? Male, female? Old, young? Is it all middle-aged women looking for a successor to Mr Rochester?"

Gregory's tone, pre-feminist-revolution as it so often was, irritated Gillian. She flinched.

"All ages, both sexes. But she does seem to have a particular appeal to the young."

As if to illustrate her words, Gregory watched as a young black man, two rows down, reached up into his Adidas bag on the rack, took out a copy of *The Black Byre*, and settled down to read it.

At the far end of the carriage Mr Rupert Coggenhoe, author of *Starveacre*, made himself comfortable for the journey north to Leeds. He had glanced at the headlines of his *Daily Telegraph* ("Major is not his own man, says Thatcher") before noting which newspapers and which books his fellow travellers in Standard Class were reading. This was normal practice for the professional author, and Rupert Coggenhoe was a very professional author indeed. He had written, as Jed Parker, novels about money, power and autopilot sex when Jeffrey Archer was in vogue. He had written, as Chantalle Derivaux, a steamy saga of sex, glitz and the fashion industry. He had written a chronicle of working-class Bootle, and, going further back, had even written books about a sexy secret agent and historical novels about various pathetic or fascinating royal ladies (*Fair Rosamund, The Swan Neck*). He had, in fact, so many aliases that his real name was known only to his agent and to his immediate neighbours in Luton. He was a professional writer, and he sold very respectably.

Respectably, however, was not how he wanted to sell. He yearned to sell in millions. He coveted special displays in W. H. Smiths, queues down Piccadilly when he signed in Hatchards, appearances on Wogan, special interviews in the colour supplements. The fact that these desiderata had never come his way he blamed on his agent, his editor, the distribution side at his publishers, and above all the publicity people. So hopeless were these last ("They couldn't sell ice-cream in the Sahara desert" he used to say) that he was forced to arrange most of the publicity for his books himself. But even then his fluent tongue and rather distinguished profile didn't secure anything but reluctant media interest.

Now he settled himself down, feet projecting out into the gangway, and read a copy of *Starveacre*, the book held poised so as to be visible to people as they made their way to the buffet. Two carriages down, in a seat with her back to the engine, his wife did exactly the same, making sure that the title was visible to those on their way back from the buffet. That was what she had been told to do, and that was what she did.

Detective Constable Dexter ("Charlie") Peace was getting a trifle bored with *The Black Byre*. He had fetched it down when he did because he had been listening in to the conversation of the young couple some seats down from him, and it suited his sense of drama to do it just at that moment. In any case he had to get as many as possible of the Sneddons' works read. He had moderately enjoyed *The Barren Fields*, had been slightly less enthusiastic about *Orchard's End*, and was now becoming bored with *The Black Byre*. He was finding the absence of irony or any other sort of humour rather oppressive. Life with Susannah can hardly have been a bundle of laughs. He imagined her as so whole-hearted, so breathlessly committed, so devoted in her relationships that he himself would have run a mile from her. To be loved by such a woman would be sheer hell.

Mind you, he'd been interested in the Introduction to *The Black Byre*, which had given details of the murder-suicide that he had not come across before. Now if he had been investigating *that* business he'd have known exactly what to do: what steps he'd have to take to check that what *seemed* to have happened was what actually happened; what weight to give to the various experts' reports; how to present his own report.

He would have been able, too, to make his own judgments on the people involved, and that would be the most interesting part. The fact that Joshua Sneddon, after murdering his sister, had drunk a cup of tea, smoked a cigarette and (according to the Introduction he had just read) stubbed out the cigarette on his dead sister's bare arm seemed to him immensely significant: this was not just an intense fit of jealousy but a hideous subterranean rage that had been boiling and seething in him for years. A rage that persisted even after murder had to be a terrible thing indeed. No, the deaths of the Sneddons he could have coped with, taken completely in his stride.

Whereas the Sneddon-related matter he was now sent on and which he had just been to London to discuss at Scotland Yard was so vague and nebulous as to approach the invisible, and the instructions were hardly more than that he maintain a watching brief. What he would do when he arrived at Batley Bridge, what he would hope to find in Micklewike and what he should do if he found it — about all these things he was uncertain.

Still, one thing he did know: the girl from two rows down would be there. He studied the pair. The man was gangling, carefree, perhaps a little pleased with himself. The girl on the other hand had in her eyes something — what was it? — something predatory, something at any rate very determined, very insistent on getting her own way. He didn't feel they made a couple. Much more, they made a contrast.

One other thing was certain: he would have to be able to talk knowledgeably, if not intelligently, about the works of Susannah Sneddon. (The works of her brother, he gathered, were in the nature of optional extras, and from the accounts he had read of them he was profoundly glad they were.) So, reverie over, he settled down once again to *The Black Byre*. The heroine had just heard heavy breathing from the hay loft.

Mrs Letitia Farraday, widow of the late Howard C. Farraday III, sat firmly ensconced in an almost empty first class compartment, her luggage around and above her. The porter had been friendly and respectful, scenting American money. He had not been disappointed.

The first class of British Rail was its usual somnolent, antechamber-to-death self, though at the far end a besuited young man was holding forth in chain-saw tones to a lookalike about financial matters. From the fragments of conversation that penetrated down to her Mrs Farraday gathered that he had been a teenage millionaire, and had lost much of it in the Wall Street slump of 'eighty-seven. She shook her head. Young people had not been thus when she had been a girl in this country.

For though the porter had been right in scenting American money, he had been wrong in assuming that Mrs Farraday herself was American, except by adoption, accent and passport. She had grown up in the North of England. Though she would never have used the phrase herself, she was now coming home.

She had been coming back to Britain every

three or four years since her second husband died, but the truth was she had no particular feeling for the country — felt happier twinges of anticipation those years when she was going to Venice, Paris or Scandinavia. She had enjoyed times in Edinburgh, North Wales and York, liked London less and less as it became progressively shabbier and more traffic-logged, and tried to avoid it. But in general she felt she could cope with anywhere on earth, could make her way without panic or disaster in all five continents.

"I am a citizen of the world," she would tell herself complacently. And she would add: "Not bad at seventy-five."

And now she was going home. She had never wanted to before, had felt no urge to retrace her steps. She had quarrelled with her parents and had quit the atmosphere of Bible and biliousness which had been the dominant notes of her childhood. She had sent them a postcard from New York in 1939, with her address on it, but they had never replied. New York had seemed heaven to her, but it would have been Sodom and Gomorrah to them. No doubt at some stage they had died, and been buried, but Letitia Farraday had no idea when, or by whom. Presumably a cousin had done the decent thing, for she had no living brothers or sisters.

Why then had that article in *Time* magazine been so evocative, why had it tugged her so strongly back to the bleak little village for which she felt no affection? There was the Sneddon connection, of course, though she had not been fond of Susannah, and had found Joshua distant and rather odd. The idea of a Weekend, or Conference, or some kind of jamboree in the old farmhouse had certainly appealed to her. *Time* magazine, ever alive to trends, had perhaps played it up a bit: her travel agent reported that it would be a distinctly modest affair. But in spite of the sub-standard accommodation which was all the area afforded, and in spite of being conscious that there were few if any of her village contemporaries she particularly wanted to meet again, she was distinctly looking forward to this weekend.

Perhaps it was the fact that she had something to contribute. Perhaps it was because, though she had told no one in advance, she was one person who really knew the Sneddons, and remembered in some detail the life they had led.

Letitia Farraday, in some corner of her amiable mind, anticipated with pleasure being a woman of importance.

★ ★ ★

When the InterCity 125 drew into platform five of Leeds Station most of the passengers streamed towards the ticket barrier, while a few clustered under the flickering indicators, trying to work out which platform to go to. Charlie Peace cast an eye over them, wondering which would turn out to be conferees: a cherubic young man who might be a clergyman in mufti — maybe; a tweedy woman with a West Highland terrier — hardly; a large American lady with a willing porter in tow — quite probably, because as he strode past them he heard the name of Micklewike, though as he looked back he saw them heading for the exit.

As he headed down the steps for platform nine Charlie saw something that intrigued him. The man whom he had seen reading *Starveacre* on his way to the buffet had met up with the woman he had seen reading *Starveacre* on his way back from the buffet. No, not met up — been reunited with. And together they were kissing in parental fashion a sulky, nondescript young woman in a college scarf who was leading them in the direction he was going himself. No, not nondescript really: actually quite pretty. But decidedly morose, and not more than dutifully pleased to see her parents. Well, actu-

33

ally not even that.

On the little sprinter train to Batley Bridge near Micklewike, which limped rather than sprinted, Charlie positioned himself not too far from them, and kept his ears open. At one point he heard the girl say:

"You're just *using* her. Capitalising on her popularity."

And he heard the father reply:

"Not at all, my dear. You know nothing whatsoever about it. Susannah Sneddon was a literary forebear, an honoured predecessor. I am merely paying my tribute."

It was said with the utmost complacency. Charlie was staggered: he would never have believed that there were people in the world who could talk in that way. Whatever else this inaugural conference of the Sneddon Fellowship threw up, it certainly seemed likely to display character types quite new to his experience. They could well turn out to be grisly beyond his imagining.

Chapter 3

Encounters

In the dignified but bland stone house on the Haworth Road which led eastwards out of Batley Bridge Charlie Peace set out his belongings. He had decided on a bed and breakfast place, as being the most likely accommodation for someone in his age group. The man who had let him in had done the usual double-take on realizing that the cockney voice he had talked to on the phone when the room was booked turned out to come from a black face. Charlie occasionally used the line "Sorry about being black — I should have warned you," accompanied by his most ferocious smile, but on this occasion the man had seemed welcoming enough, and Charlie on his present mission had every reason not to make waves.

Now, in the attractive, chintzy bedroom, he unpacked his things: hung up his most conservative suit, put in the drawers his white and striped shirts (God! how fed up he was with striped shirts, but what else could you get these days?) and set out on top of the chest his light portable typewriter. He was aiming to use any spare time this weekend to improve his typing, which he was the first to admit was ludicrously ham-fisted. He was also intending to make a written record of every impression, oddity or ambiguity that came through to him over the weekend. He felt it was going to be that sort of a case — if, indeed, it turned out to be a case at all. Now he slipped a piece of paper into the machine and typed: "The quick brown fox jumped over the lazy dog." Then he put the wooden shield over the keys, set out the key guide, and typed it again: "The wuick brown foz jumped over the laxy dog." Three mistakes. Not bad. Not good either.

He knotted the sleeves of a pullover round his neck, for by now he knew Yorkshire weather and had a healthy mistrust of its sun. Then he patted his trouser pocket for money and the front door key and left his room, bounding down the stairs. On an impulse, and hearing noises from the kitchen, he went down the hallway and poked his head round the door.

"Hello — sorry to bother you: I'm your

b. and b. man," he said to the plump woman at the sink. "I was wondering if it will be all right if I should decide to stay until Monday. If the weather's good I might decide to do a bit of walking."

"Oh yes, that should be all right. I'm Mrs Ludlum, by the way. We don't have many bookings this time of year. We have our regulars, but they're mostly in the school holidays. In April and May it's mostly casuals sent from the Tourist Office. If you could tell me Sunday breakfast time, so I don't give the room to anyone else during the day."

"I will . . . Where do you think most of the Sneddon Weekend people will be staying?"

"Oh, all over. You're lucky we had this room these two nights — we had a cancellation. Most bed and breakfast places are full for tonight and tomorrow, and so is the Duke of Cumberland. That's where you'll find the best part of them, at the Cumberland. It's got fifteen or twenty rooms. Turn left when you go out the front door, and when you come to the town centre it's the big, sprawling pub painted white."

Charlie smiled his thanks, and made tracks back to the town centre. The Duke of Cumberland was indeed sprawling, but its very ramshackle structure made it attractive. Several drinkers were sitting outside in the watery, early-evening sun, many in plaid shirts and heavy boots. Charlie scented conference-goers and decided to join them, but as he was getting his pint of Bodington's from the bar he felt a hand on his arm.

"Young man, do you think you could be so kind as to take my glass over to a table? It's difficult hobbling with a stick and a glass as well."

The voice was American. He turned and saw the large woman he had seen on Leeds station. Her hand was firmly grasping the head of her stick, and a determined but friendly expression was on her face. A woman who knew her own mind and would speak it, he decided: someone who would despise meanness and double-dealing. A fair woman.

"Sure," he said. "Need my arm as well?"

"No, no. I manage, I manage. It's worse than usual tonight. I got a bit stiff on the long train journey from London, and then in the taxi from Leeds."

Taxi from Leeds! Charlie thought. Well, no ride in a scruffy little Sprinter train for this lady. Almost certainly one of the conference-goers, he thought: a rich American enthusiast.

"Will this do?" he asked as she hobbled

behind him to a corner table with a good view down the length of the bar. "Do you want to be alone, or would you mind if I joined you?"

"I'd be delighted if you would join me, and I never want to be alone. I've been alone all too much since my second husband died. You'll know how strange and unpleasant that can be, young man, if you ever are widowed."

"Haven't even managed to get a wife yet," grinned Charlie, as they settled down on the sofa seats that gave them the best view. "Not that I'm at the Weekend to find one. I don't think Susannah Sneddon's novels are an encouragement to matrimony."

"Ah, so you're at the Conference, are you? Or jamboree, or Weekend, or Celebration, or whatever we are to call it." There was a light scepticism in her tone that made Charlie revise his estimate of her as an enthusiast. Perhaps she recognised in him a kindred spirit, a fellow-ironist, for she continued: "Now offhand I wouldn't have picked you as a literary enthusiast or a culture vulture."

Charlie blinked, recognising the idea he had had of the conferees as birds of prey.

"There have got to be a few surprises in the pack," he replied in neutral tones. "Still, looking around this bar I feel I could pick the Sneddon people."

"So do I: there, there, there and there." She had launched a sweeping gaze over the drinkers and then pointed unobtrusively to four of them — just the ones that Charlie would himself have picked.

"Right," he said. "And just possibly there. But we're probably entirely wrong. And even if we're right, it's not all that clever, because the locals mark themselves out by the way they behave, and there aren't that many left."

"Thank you for that douche of cold water on my self-esteem, young man."

"Anyway, what do people who attend literary do's like this look like?"

The woman set down her glass after a hefty swig.

"You're asking me? I've never been to one in my life. It's not my sort of scene at all. I've got a friend who goes, though — Thomas Hardy, Jane Austen, that kind of thing. She says that you get all ages and types, but that what is common to most of them is a sort of mild mania."

"Sounds nasty."

"It can make them very quarrelsome, she says. They've got themselves fixated on this one author, often for some odd, personal reason. Some of them hardly read any other author, just madly re-read the one."

"Slightly unbalanced, she means? I don't think of myself as slightly unbalanced."

"Give it time, young man. Think of those people who go through the Sherlock Holmes stories as if they were literal fact, finding mad reasons for all the contradictions, whereas really it was just Conan Doyle forgetting what he'd written years earlier. And by the way, it's not just literary obsessions that grow into something a little mad. My friend says there's a Richard III Society full of people who never read any history except the life and times of Richard, and only that to show that he was a saint on earth."

Charlie raised his eyebrows.

"The inference being that you've got to be a bit dotty to join one of these specialist societies?"

"Too right — or so my friend says. And we are to be founder-members of a new dottiness, as you call it."

"Right," agreed Charlie. "A sobering thought." Then he incautiously asked the very question that he hoped she wasn't going to ask him. "What got you hooked on Susannah Sneddon?"

The American woman swigged again at her gin and tonic.

"I'm not. I read one years ago, and another

on the plane coming over. Competent enough, but not my cup of tea."

"Joshua, then?"

"Gahd, no! I'd better explain. I come from Micklewike. I was born and brought up there."

Charlie's face expressed his surprise.

"So you're not American?"

"American*ised*. I feel American. England is a foreign country to me, though I visit it fairly often. But I thought I'd come back to Micklewike just for once, before it gets too late . . ." She seemed just about to get started on her explanation when she caught sight of someone at the door and her jaw dropped. "Good Lord! Heathcliff!"

Charlie's eyes followed hers to the door that led to the foyer and Reception. A tall, dark man in a sombre tweed jacket had come into the bar. His sharply chiselled features and erect bearing bore the stamp of command, or at any rate personal arrogance, and his body proclaimed him sturdy country stock.

"I can't find anyone at Reception," he said, in ringing tones to the woman behind the bar. His voice had money in it, though perhaps not old money.

"Oh no, lovey. We have to double up at opening times. Just let me finish this order

42

and I'll be with you."

The man let his eyebrows rise a fraction, but he turned and went back to the foyer.

"Not Heathcliff," said Charlie. "Too smooth. More like some kind of guards officer."

"Well, perhaps I do mean Hollywood Heathcliff. Have you ever seen the film with the young Olivier? All brilliantine and beautiful voice? That sort of Heathcliff."

"A conference attender, would you say?"

"I didn't see the light of madness in his eyes. But then, I didn't with you, young man."

"Charlie — Charlie Peace."

"I'm Lettie Farraday. And now I've finished this drink I'm going to go up to Micklewike to my old home. I do wonder if I'm mad: I always hated the place."

"You're not going to walk it?"

"Hell, no. I'll get them to call me a cab."

"I'll get them to call you one from the bar," said Charlie, getting up. "I'm going up myself, but I'd rather walk."

"There's a path up from the Pack Horse Bridge, or there was in my day. That path! I did it so often it was a matter of course, but it's a back-breaker. If we meet up at the village I'll buy you a drink. You'll need it."

There was no one behind the bar when Charlie got to it, and he rang for a taxi from the phone in the foyer. He was only a couple of feet away from the darkly handsome man who was bent over the reception desk registering himself in. His suitcase was by his side, and Charlie could see an old airline tag tied around the handle. It bore the name Randolph Sneddon.

The path up to Micklewike was every bit as backbreaking as Lettie Farraday had said it was — steep, cobbled, with only a rusty old handrail for support. When he reached the point where it bisected the road Charlie paused and looked over the rolling Yorkshire hills, dotted with disused mills and clusters of houses: grand, inspiring, but hell to walk in, he thought.

Then, as he paused to recuperate, another thought occurred to him: how old was Lettie Farraday? She was well-preserved, apart from her lameness, but he would still put her definitely into her seventies. What would that make her birth date? Say 1915, or a bit later. That would mean that if she grew up in Micklewike she could have known Susannah Sneddon and her brother Joshua. No — it was such a small place it would mean that she *would* have known them. It was

44

hardly one of those legendary conjunctures that make the heart stop, like meeting someone who had survived the sinking of the *Titanic*, or someone who had watched Queen Victoria's funeral, but nevertheless it was interesting, suggestive . . .

Charlie looked up at the continuation of the path: daunting, and starting with a long flight of steps. The road might take longer, but it would certainly be easier. When he had been walking along it for nearly ten minutes he realized that he might not be going in the right direction. He grinned wryly at himself for a city boy. When he came to another path, gentler, which claimed to lead to Micklewike he turned gratefully up it, and five minutes later he landed up, through an overgrown back lane, in one of the cobbled side-streets of Susannah Sneddon's home village. His calf and thigh muscles shouldn't be aching, he thought, but they undoubtedly were.

Charlie was getting used to Yorkshire villages. When he had first come to live and work in Leeds and the West Yorkshire area he had found them unsettling — had felt an intruder there. It was not just his colour but his London accent that had made him stand out and feel foreign. Now he had accustomed himself to them and to his feeling of foreignness, and he was happy to acknowledge that Micklewike was an exceptionally interesting and well-preserved example. Set on the brow of a hill, horribly exposed to wind and weather, it seemed to bear its history lightly but proudly. The main street wound up towards open countryside, and off it poky little cobbled lanes edged with cottages led to a chapel, the parish church, or quite often to nowhere very much. Other tourists and conference-goers were wandering around, giving it a more peopled air than it would normally have, Charlie guessed. He made for the church first, and found that it was in fact two — a ruined one and a stolid Victorian one separated only by a churchyard. He lounged around looking at the gravestones, noting the names that kept recurring: Greenwoods, Arkwrights, Hobsons. He saw no Sneddons, but he had no doubt they were there somewhere, and that the graves would be visited over the weekend. Or had they, having no children, been buried in unmarked graves and the place forgotten?

He went back to the main street and toiled up to the top. Somewhere just beyond where the village ended must lie High Maddox Farm. Ahead of him he saw a gate with a girl leaning on it, gazing into the horizon: that would surely be it. As he approached he realized it was the girl he had seen on Leeds station with her parents.

"Hi," he said. She turned and smiled, losing the look of discontent for a moment and showing an attractive approachability.

"Hi."

"This is it, then, is it?" Charlie asked, leaning over the gate beside her and looking towards the low, bleak farmhouse approached by a mean little dirt track. "That's where they lived . . ." He turned his eyes towards a clump of trees further in the distance. "And that, I suppose, is where Joshua shot himself?"

"Do you think a lot of this interest is a bit *News of the World*?" the girl asked suddenly. "I mean, say she'd just gone on churning out that sort of book till she died naturally, would there be the *same* interest?"

"Don't know," said Charlie simply. Then he thought for a moment. "Murder gets people in. No point in feeling superior about it: it always does. And there's another thing: I think maybe that if she'd gone on writing novels like that for another twenty years or so, there'd have been too many of them. As it is they get a bit — "

"Samey. Yes, that's what I think."

"Why are you here then?"

"Oh, my parents were coming here, and

as I'm at university in Leeds they dragged me along."

"Reluctantly, by the sound of it."

The girl pouted.

"I think my father wants to make publicity for himself out of all this."

"Publicity? How come? Is he a Sneddon or something?"

"Oh no, but he is a writer. I think he wants to generate a bit of publicity for himself: him as Susannah Sneddon's present-day successor."

"Does he write rural-passion novels?"

"He writes all sorts. He's very versatile. He has to be because he's not very good at any one thing. Oh God, I sound like a bitch, don't I?"

"If you can't bitch about your own parents, who can you bitch about? Your father didn't by any chance write a book called *Starveacre*, did he?"

"Yes. It's pretty rotten. Why?"

"Oh, nothing. Feel like a drink?"

The girl brightened up, then looked at her watch and screwed up her face.

"I'd have loved to, but I'll have to go down the hill. They keep me on a very short leash when I'm around them, which is silly because I've got away from them now, haven't I? Dad is giving interviews to the *Keighley Advertiser* and the *Bradford Telegraph and Argus* — big deal, eh? — but he said he'd be free at eight, and then we'd all go and have dinner somewhere. I'd prefer a hamburger, but being interviewed always makes Dad rather stately, so I expect it'll be the plushiest restaurant in town, and probably ghastly heavy food."

"With a bit of luck he'll find there isn't any plushy restaurant in Batley Bridge. It isn't that sort of place. What about tomorrow? A drink after the jamboree?"

"I'd love that. Where? The pub down the road?"

"Where Joshua Sneddon mooned into his pint pot and meditated his tiny sales — where else?"

"See you there."

She smiled again, waved, and began the walk down the hill. Charlie thought he could get to like her, then remembered he had not even asked her name, or where she was staying. He turned back and gazed towards the farm. Starveacre, indeed! It would have been that sort of place in the Sneddons' time, made worse by Joshua's lack of aptitude for farming. Probably it had been madly prosperous in more recent times, rolling in Common Market subsidies. It wouldn't be surprising if the farmer had built himself more commodious and less gloomy accommodation elsewhere, and sold off this place to someone connected to the Sneddon Society. Except that the Society — or Fellowship, or whatever they decided to call themselves — was not yet constituted. To the interesting Mr Gerald Suzman, then. He was presumably the owner at the present time.

Meditating on the little he knew about the said Gerald Suzman, Charlie turned and began the walk down the main street towards the Black Horse.

Lettie Farraday's walk around Micklewike was less carefree than Charlie's, burdened as it was with memories and associations. She told the taxi driver to take her to High Maddox Farm, gave him a splendid tip, and told him to come back to the Black Horse in two hours' time. Like Charlie she leaned over the gate, in her case not to speculate but to get her memories in order. Then she started heavily down the hill.

The main street and the occasional cobbled alleyway off it had no charms for her. She disliked the grimy stone, the four-square style of building, the pokiness of the cottages — each pokiness joined to the next pokiness in a mean little row. Those places would still be dark and cramped, though nothing like as dark and cramped as had been the one that was her home. She had a vision of herself, her father and mother and the brother who had died of pneumonia all cooped up together night after dark night, eating coarse food off chipped plates on ugly sticks of furniture. Anything beautiful her parents had classed as a 'vanity'. Almost anything that wasn't basic and plain was a 'vanity'. On an impulse she turned aside and went towards the Methodist Chapel. There the family had worshiped, when they had not gone to a sect still more narrow and doom-laden in Batley Bridge. The Micklewike Chapel had once been an attractive octagonal building, but it was marred by an added section at the back. That's the trouble with Nonconformity, Lettie thought: no *style*.

Back in the main street she stood for a moment at the end of the alleyway that included her own family hovel. She remembered the atmosphere: obsessive scrubbings, nightly Bible-readings by gas lamp, continual hectoring reproofs, spankings for small or imagined naughtinesses. Had things changed in the house, she wondered? They could only have changed for the better.

As she watched her old front door opened. An elderly woman in a tweed skirt and cardigan came out, called "Just popping down to Alice's for a few minutes" into the house, then marched past her without a second glance. Change indeed! The house is now a retirement home for a middle-class couple, Lettie thought. Could it be that people are happy there?

She went slowly towards the churchyard and found the spot where her brother was buried. He was the only living thing in her home for whom she had had affection. She had loved him, passionately. When he had died she had known immediately that she would leave. Nothing could bind her to this place, these people. She stood for a moment by the spot, remembering him. Then, as tears came to her eyes, she turned and hobbled painfully back towards the main street, wishing she had not come.

"I'm an old fool," she berated herself bitterly. "Coming back to *this*."

She paused for breath when she regained the tarmac, and looking down towards the Black Horse she saw that Charlie Peace was standing in the doorway with a pint glass in his hand. She cast one more look up the street, then back at the alley where she was born, and was about to turn down towards Charlie and the company of the living when she realized that an old woman coming down the street was looking at her curiously.

"I know you, don't I?" the woman said. "Or used to, any road."

Lettie felt herself gripped by a reluctance to take up with her past, but she did not like lying.

"You could do," she said. "I grew up here."

"Lettie Blatchley!" said the woman triumphantly. "I can still make out your features. I'm Milly Winkworth. I were the year after you in school."

"I think I remember the name . . ."

"I used to be a bit sweet on your brother."

"A lot of girls were."

"Well, you *have* done well for yourself, I can see that. Folk sometimes said as how you had, but no one really knew. Come for this weekend do, have you?"

"Yes, I have. Rather on an impulse. I don't know why."

The woman looked at her conspiratorially.

"Never thought owt to the Sneddons in our day, did we?" She said it in the reductive way some Yorkshire people have. "She were a bit of a slut, that's what folk said. And we thought the books were mucky."

"Perhaps we were wrong," said Lettie, finding the woman's attitude distasteful. "Perhaps we were a bit jealous because she

53

did write things, did get them published, did get known."

"Happen. Any road, it's a good thing for the village." She nodded down the hill in the direction of the Black Horse. "Mike Bradshaw says he's never known so many tourists and gawpers."

Lettie Farraday smiled a farewell that was also a dismissal.

"Very nice for him. I hope he makes the most of it. I'm a tourist and a gawper now, and I'm going to join them."

It was as she was turning away that the woman lobbed her a question that stunned her like a blow from a club.

"You'll be going up to see yer Mam, will you?"

Chapter 4

The Black Horse

It was Charlie who bore the brunt. When he saw Lettie Farraday, white with shock, tottering towards him down the hill, saw her shoulders heaving with barely suppressed sobs, he went forward, put his arm around her, and supported her into the Saloon Bar of the Black Horse. He found a dark corner free of tourists or locals and let her sink into a sofa seat.

"Brandy," he said firmly. "That's what you need. And have a good cry if you want to. Nobody's paying any attention to you."

That wasn't entirely true. As he went up to the bar to get the brandy he saw several people casting glances at Lettie out of the corners of their eyes. Her clothes, her make-up marked her out as not English. Some of the elderly locals were creasing their foreheads, and some of those who were clearly in the area for the Sneddon Weekend were already eyeing off the drinkers to work out who was there on the same mission. In any case an elderly woman in a state of shock and weeping in the corner of a pub will always arouse attention, usually of a contemptuous kind.

"Right — get this down you," said Charlie, putting the double brandy down in front of her. "And then have another if you feel the need."

"I shall feel the need," said Lettie with conviction. "What an old fool I am . . . But then, it was such a shock, you see. Such an *awful* surprise."

Charlie kept quiet, not wanting to seem inquisitorial. But when she looked up he raised his eyebrows.

"I mean, I assumed they'd died years ago."

"Who?"

"My parents. Believe me, I would *never* have come back here if I'd known."

"You'd had no contact since you went to America?"

"I did send them a postcard in . . . in 1939 it would have been. To give them an address and tell them I was married. That was my first husband, and his name was Ciesinski. To tell you the truth, I knew a name like that would send them into fits.

Not English, probably a Catholic, sure signs that I'd gone irretrievably to the devil. So I knew they'd never contact me . . . I was glad. I suppose I really sent the card to say I was all right and that all was over between us. But they must have known that. I would *never* . . . Oh God, stop me when I keep saying that."

Charlie was pleased to see she seemed to be regaining some spirit. Self-mockery was a good sign.

"Anyhow, now you find they're still alive?"

"My mother. Just my mother. That woman out there says she's in some kind of home at Hipperholt. That's twenty miles north. She said it with a knowing, malicious kind of smile on her face. She must have known it would be a horrible shock."

"But if your mother is alive . . . I don't know how to put this tactfully — "

"She must be as old as Methuselah? Right. You don't have to be tactful with me, young man. I'm seventy-five. My mother was twenty-four when she had me. Jesus Christ! Next year she'll be getting a telegram from the Queen! She'll complain that she didn't bring it herself! Well, just so long as they don't expect me to be around to pose with her for the photographers!" She paused to sip her brandy. "Good Lord — what must you think of an old woman who cries when she finds her mother is still alive?"

Charlie shrugged.

"If I like the old woman, I decide that the mother must have been a bit of a monster."

Lettie Farraday considered.

"Monster? No, not that. Narrow, bigoted, hard, joyless . . . I had a childhood in which there was no joy . . . I felt nothing for her — either of them — because they couldn't love. You have to be taught love; it's not a one-way process. I loved my brother. When he died I got out."

"What did they do, your parents?"

"My father worked on a farm down the hill. My mother was mostly at home, but she did occasional cleaning for people. She worked for the Sneddons, actually."

"She worked for the Sneddons!"

The voice came from behind Charlie's shoulder. A young couple had edged their way forward, and had been listening. Charlie had seen them in one of the old advertising mirrors on the wall, but as Lettie didn't seem to object he had said nothing. He had recognised them as the young couple he had heard talking on the train, and now he looked at Lettie to see if she wanted them given their marching orders. But she seemed well on the road to recovery, and not displeased by the attention.

"Oh yes, every Thursday. Sweeping, dusting scouring. Susannah Sneddon was a bit of a slattern. It was hard work because everything was so dirty, and they didn't have vacuum cleaners or running hot water or anything like that. They did towards the end have electricity, which marked them off from most people in the village. That was so that they could write in the evenings comfortably. My mother liked hard physical work. It made her feel good. It made her grimmer as she erased every stain and chased dirt in every corner. She thought how grubby other people were, and how inferior to herself. Cleaning houses gave her a sort of perverted spiritual pleasure."

The girl behind Charlie had been drinking in every word. She now leaned over his shoulder, an expression of intense interest on her face, or rather, an expression of something more than interest: she was drinking all this in, like a leech sucking blood. Charlie shifted uneasily in his seat, but the girl insisted on introducing herself.

"I'm Gillian Parkin. I'm writing my Ph.D. thesis on Susannah Sneddon. This is my boyfriend Gregory Waite. He's not really a Sneddon person."

"Well, hi, Gregory! You and me both," said Lettie Farraday, a full return of her old spirit.

"You can't mean that!" wailed Gillian. "You knew them. You must have so much knowledge that you can share with the rest of us!"

Lettie shrugged.

"Have I? I used to go up with my mother sometimes in the school holidays. But look: say the person you were writing your thesis on was Browning, and you went along to a séance and got in touch with the woman who did his rough cleaning. How much of interest do you think she'd have to tell you?"

"I'd be interested in what kind of porridge he had for breakfast," said Gillian stoutly. "And you saw her, you know what she looked like."

"There are photographs — there's a good one on the back of *Orchard's End*."

"But photographs then were usually posed," put in Gregory Waite quietly. "What kind of physical impression did she make?"

Lettie Farraday considered.

"Not altogether pleasant. But I may be confusing physical impression with something else. You see normally when I went up there with my mother Susannah would be out walking — I suppose she organised it like that, so that the day the house was cleaned was her day for thinking and planning. She might come in just before we finished, and let my mother make us all a cup of tea, though she never had any conversation much, or any interest in how we lived. But if she did happen to be writing that day she'd bundle us off upstairs, insist on quiet — well, to a young girl it all seemed a bit pretentious."

"What about the physical impression?" persisted Gregory.

"Heavy. Or rather running to heaviness. There was something quite attractive about the face, and perhaps there once had been about the body too. She rather let herself go. She wouldn't be the only girl who had had her emotional life ruined by the First World War. I'm trying to be fair, you see, but to my young eyes there was something else — a sort of self-regard, a feeling of being different from the rest of us, that she cherished. That didn't help to make her more attractive to me."

"Did you hear of any boyfriends?"

"None. I suppose she could have found herself a husband if she'd wanted to."

"Why do you say that?" Charlie asked.

"She earned money — not bad money. There was a lot of talk about that in the village. Someone saw a cheque from a publisher for two hundred pounds. A farm worker in a tied cottage was taking home a weekly wage in shillings not pounds at that time. It seemed to us an immense sum, just for writing."

"And yet the farm was such a poor place."

"Joshua wasn't much of a farmer."

"Did the money go to the farm, do you think?"

"I've no idea. It could have done, if Susannah wanted to stay put, like Emily Brontë never being happy away from Haworth. But I can't say she ever showed any great love for the farm itself, only for the countryside around."

"Was it your mother saw the cheque and spread the gossip?" asked Charlie.

"I shouldn't think so. My mother — with all her faults, and they were legion — wasn't one for gossip. She never had the sort of friends you need to gossip *with*. Oh God — why did you bring her up? What am I going to *do?*"

She looked beseechingly at Charlie.

"Do you want to see her?" he asked

"*No* . . . Oh, I don't know. I never for a moment imagined the question would come up."

"Don't you even have the sort of grisly curiosity that asks: 'What on earth will she be like at ninety-nine?' I'm afraid I would."

"Well . . ." Lettie shot him a quick, humorous glance. "I do rather think I would like to *see*."

"She may be in the sort of state where it makes no difference one way or the other. She might not know you."

"No . . . I suppose I could ring the Home."

"That's what I was thinking. On the other hand she may be mentally very spry."

"Oh God! Spare me! She'll probably lecture me on my wicked ways. I'm too *old* to get involved with that kind of thing."

"You could have a nice ding-dong row," Charlie suggested.

"No — *she's* too old for me to involve her in that."

"But what is — was — your mother like?" asked Gillian.

"Young lady," said Lettie, leaning forwards, "I left home at fifteen and went to America at twenty, and since then, beyond a postcard, I have never tried to communicate with her. I think that tells you all you need to know about what I think of her, *and* how welcome she is as a topic of conversation. *Now*" — she looked at her watch — "I think my taxi will be waiting. Are you intending to walk down the hill, as well as up, Charlie?"

"Not if a better way presents itself. One of the things I've learnt since coming to Yorkshire is that steep hills are as gruelling down as they are up."

"Whoever would have thought anything else? You can come with me and help me up to my room."

She looked enquiringly at the young pair.

"I'm staying here," said Gillian.

"And I'm sleeping on the floor, and taking off tomorrow to get away from all this Sneddonry," said Gregory.

"Then I'll say goodbye to you, and goodnight to you, young lady. We shall no doubt talk — or at any rate see each other — during the Weekend."

"Did I rather slap her down?" she asked Charlie in the taxi.

"Not really. You made it clear the subject is a painful one. She's bright, if a bit intense. She will have understood."

"Hmmm — intense she was. It's that mania we talked about."

At the door to her room Mrs Farraday turned to thank Charlie.

"I'm sure you've had more than you'll have wanted of an old lady's company for one day. I've got a lot of hard thinking to do. But I want you to know I'm grateful, Charlie, I really am . . . Charlie Peace: didn't your mother know about the murderer?"

Charlie grinned. It was an old question.

"Don't blame my mother. It's a nickname. My real name is Dexter."

"Dexter! Now that's a nice name. I once had an American friend called Dexter. I shall call you that."

Charlie had noticed, in the course of the evening, that Lettie Farraday's speech had become less American, more English, and even more Yorkshire. That obviously had not meant a lessening of affection for things American. Coming to Yorkshire was not, for Lettie, coming home. It was being away from home.

Charlie clattered down the stairs to the foyer, intending to go straight back to his room in the Haworth Road. But as he passed the door into the bar he saw the darkly handsome man who had arrived earlier, now standing at the crowded bar trying to catch the barmaid's attention. On an impulse he swerved aside, went into the bar and managed to stand beside him.

"Diabolical service," he said, when the man had failed to get noticed yet again. "You'd think they'd have put more staff on for the Conference."

The man turned to look at him. The expression on his full, regular features said as clearly as words that neither Charlie's accent nor his colour qualified him for friendly notice. Charlie knew the expression well.

"You would," he said shortly, and turned away. Obviously a thought struck him, for he turned back. "Are you here for the Conference?"

"That's right."

The man smiled, though still with a certain aloofness. He was motivated, probably, by nothing more than some dim sense of *Sneddon oblige*. While he condescended Charlie caught the girl's attention.

"Oh, miss, an orange juice, please. And what are you having?"

"Scotch and soda. I'll pay, of course. You seem to be better than me at getting noticed." Charlie smiled ambiguously. He thought that with looks like that Sneddon wouldn't often have a problem. "No, I must say I'm feeling a bit apprehensive about this Conference."

They had moved away from the bar, but not sat down. Charlie felt that sitting down with this man, now fumbling for the price of his Scotch, would be to overestimate the thawing.

"Oh?" Charlie said, as if he had no idea who he was speaking to. "But you're going?"

"Yes," he said, his expression rueful, almost shamefaced. "I'm the nearest living relative."

"*Really!*" Charlie's voice and bearing suggested that he was enormously impressed. "So you're representing the family?"

"I *am* the family. But I'm not looking forward to being among all those culture vultures and devoted fans. I really know nothing whatever about the books."

"Not admired in the family?"

"Hardly ever mentioned, frankly. I grew up knowing I had some sort of cousin who'd once written novels, and that was about it. Once all this stuff about a Society or Fellowship or whatever started up I sat down and read a couple of the books — had to discipline myself and set aside two evenings when I'd very much rather have been doing something else."

"And?"

Once more the expression was rueful.

"I found I'd very much rather have done something else. Shocking, I know. You must be an admirer."

"I find them interesting," said Charlie cautiously. "You say she was some sort of cousin . . . ?"

"Yes. My grandfather was her cousin, to be precise. But he and his family moved South long ago — well before the war. I don't even know this area, I'm afraid. I've been to Yorkshire only once in my life, and then it was to York, not to this side. So I'm afraid I'm going to be a great disappointment to the aficionados."

"They'll be thrilled just to have a member of her family here. Or their family, I should say."

"Oh God — don't mention Joshua. Just a *look* at one of his books was enough."

"Yes. They're an acquired taste I haven't acquired. But there will be fans of his too, remember."

"So I'll have to find some polite formula. Thanks for warning me. But I'm in the City. I have to be polite and tactful to all types of people. I once had lunch with Robert Maxwell and survived to tell the tale. I'll think of something . . ."

His eyes strayed around the bar. He was about to say "Well, it's been nice having this chat." Charlie drained his glass.

"Well, it's been nice having this chat. I must be off. I expect we'll see each other up in Micklewike tomorrow. Best of luck with the fans."

"Thanks, I'll need it."

Charlie dredged up from memory an O-level quote.

" 'I will see thee at Philippi.' "

Randolph Sneddon looked bewildered, as if he thought it might be the next village to Micklewike.

That night, making notes of the day's encounters, Charlie put by Sneddon's name the comment: "Not very bright." Then frowning he crossed it out, because that wasn't at all the impression the man had made as a whole. After some thought he substituted: "Sharp at some things. Money? Self-interest?" He somehow didn't think that many people would be encouraged to get close to Randolph Sneddon. He was quite sure that he wouldn't be.

Chapter 5

Inauguration

The village hall of Micklewike had been built in the 'thirties, five minutes from the centre of the village, on the edge of a small estate of council houses. Here, over the years, the local amateurs had performed *Tons of Money*, *Night Must Fall* and *Haul for the Shore* until the television habit had become so deeply ingrained that it was impossible to get the villagers out into their bleak, windswept streets for a night in a draughty hall. These were, in any case, performances more for the benefit of the actors than the audience. Nowadays there were aerobics classes held there, and karate classes, and the occasional lecture or school concert. But for much of the time the hall stood dispirited and unused. It was here that the Sneddon Fellowship was to be born.

Mr Suzman had been uncertain how many

would be attending the inaugural meeting. He had a rough idea how many were lodged in local hotels, inns and bed and breakfast places, because he liaised closely with the Batley Bridge Tourist Office. What he did not know was how many would prefer to stay at more distant places such as Haworth or Skipton, nor how many locals within easy driving distance would decide to come to the inaugural junketings. When he drove into Micklewike an hour before the meeting was scheduled to begin he was pleased to note that the meagre places for parking in the village were starting to fill up. He had a last-minute pow-wow with Mrs Marsden at the farm, then took himself down to the village hall. Here he had another pow-wow with Mrs Cardew, an elderly resident of Micklewike, whom he had persuaded to take notes at the meeting, and whom he hoped would eventually act as (unpaid) secretary to the Fellowship. For the title, and the cost of the postage, he anticipated getting a great deal of work out of her. Then he went to stand at the door of the hall, mingle with one or two familiar faces outside, and generally to act as mine host and onlie begetter of the Fellowship. But while he was welcoming and mingling outside in the watery sunlight he was all the time keeping an eye on the number and kind of people who were assembling around him in dribs and drabs, smiling tentatively at each other, and generally beginning the business of coming together.

"A nice little bunch," Gerald Suzman thought, with the part of his mind that was not commenting on the weather or pointing out landmarks from the Sneddon novels to perfect strangers. "I wouldn't mind betting we shall have sixty or seventy, and there's a fair number who are only arriving this afternoon. Ah — a member of the ethnic minorities: that always looks good. Young too — in fact it's generally a gratifyingly young lot." By which he meant that there was a scattering of genuinely young people, and that there were more under-sixties than are generally found in such societies. "What's that — German? No, not guttural enough. One of the Scandinavian languages, I should think. Oh — *very* nice! Young, but not too young, lovely long blonde hair." He was stirred by an unmistakeably lascivious urge. Mr Suzman had been a notable womanizer in his time, and his time was not yet up. He suppressed the urge as suitable neither to the time nor the place, but mentally registered an intention to engineer a time and place that was suitable. And the place wouldn't be a hedgerow or a barn, he told himself. "Down, Gerald," he said mentally to dampen his ardour. "Look at her legs. *Not* graceful. And her bearded boyfriend looks very capable. Why boyfriend? Why not husband? Scandinavians marry sometimes, I suppose. But he doesn't look like a husband, so I will hope . . . Ah — she's meeting up with another young girl. I suspect that may be the — what is it? Parker, Parkin, something like that, woman. Writes long letters full of questions, and very interested in the manuscripts. No doubt a future contributor to our journal. To be encouraged, but not allowed too close. Ten minutes to go. Yes, a very nice little group indeed. Perhaps we should all be moving inside."

As he himself began the move back to the door and into the hall people gathered around him obediently and followed: his photograph had been several times in the *Batley Bridge Advertiser*, and recently in the *Yorkshire Post*. He moved down towards the platform and his seat in the centre of it, and from it he sat surveying the people assembling. Most of them were coming down for good seats at the front, though he noticed that the young black man had taken one in the middle of one of the back rows. Diffident, he thought to himself. I must try to bring him out, bring him forward.

It did not occur to him that only from the back could one see everything that was going on.

Charlie Peace had had an early breakfast — a full Yorkshire one, with endless toast and tea — and had chatted to his landlord and landlady while he was getting it down. When they asked what had drawn him to Susannah Sneddon he said that a girlfriend had introduced him to the novels. The girlfriend had gone, but the interest had not. When they asked him what he did, he said: "Security work."

"Really? Wouldn't have thought there were many men in Security who were readers," Mrs Ludlum had said.

"Oh, I don't know," said Charlie. "Some of my mates can sit around all day with the *Sun*."

Careful, he said to himself. His sardonic humour had more than once got him into trouble when he had used it at inappropriate moments.

When he'd finished his fried feast he decided that the only thing to do after that kind of meal was to take the hill path up to Micklewike. He thought to himself that he would regard it as his daily training over the weekend, his means of keeping himself in condition. And he had to admit that, second time round, it had become easier, because you knew what you were in for.

He had prepared for his first view of Mr Gerald Suzman by remembering the various photographs he had been shown at the Yard, so the sight of the man, as he emerged from the door of the village hall at the same time as Charlie joined the group milling around outside it, was no surprise. But though the man was unmistakeable the impression made was very different: none of the photographs he had seen were informal snaps, or taken when he was off-guard, and as Gregory Waite had said the day before, a posed photograph is always the imposition of a desired impression, with greater or lesser success. In the flesh, publicly performing, Gerald Suzman was busy, ingratiating, plausible, but Charlie told himself that even if he had been watching him "cold" he would have had doubts about — what? — his sincerity? His honesty? He simply did not give the impression of a man of integrity.

He strolled nearer to him, but he caught nothing but commonplaces from his conversation with the various conferees. At first Gerald Suzman then the rest began the movement into the hall. Charlie noticed the girl he had talked to at High Maddox Farm the day before: he gave her a wave and a meaningful look and got an instant response. But she seemed firmly attached to her father and mother, and was shepherded by them to a seat in the second row. Charlie had no intention of missing what went on in the main body of the hall just for a close view of Gerald Suzman, and took an uncharacteristically inconspicuous seat at the back.

The meeting began with Gerald Suzman explaining with disarming (if you were readily disarmed) self-deprecation that he had constituted himself chairman for this inaugural meeting, and that more formal arrangements could wait until a small committee for the Fellowship had been elected and a provisional constitution adopted — of which a draft would be found on every seat. That would take place at a formal meeting on Sunday morning. Meanwhile what he hoped for from this morning's meeting was an expression of what those potential members assembled there — and how welcome they all were, and how gratifying the large number! — wanted from the Society, how they each hoped to contribute to it, how they felt the Society could best honour the memory of Susannah Sneddon — not forgetting Joshua! — and raise (to use a convenient cliché) their profile in the literary world.

So far so boring, Charlie thought. As members in the body of the hall showed signs of wishing to speak, Mr Suzman gracefully gave way and the discussion became more general. Mr Rupert Coggenhoe got up and spoke "as a writer myself, and from a writer's standpoint." He contrived to introduce the name of his novel *Starveacre*, and the pseudonym he had written it under, three times in the course of his contribution (all those rehearsals in his mind of what he would do when he became a chat-show regular thus paid some small dividends). When he sat down Charlie was hard put to remember anything he had said. A dumpy lady in a bright blue coat and hat got up and announced she was from the *Shirley* country, bemusing Charlie, who began speculating where that was in relation to Herriot country, Brontë Country and *Last of the Summer Wine* country. The lady suggested that it be written into the constitution of the Society that High Maddox Farm was never to be added to or built on to without express permission of a majority of Society members.

"An excellent idea! Capital!" enthused Mr Suzman. "Though I think we must say that the farm is never likely to be a shrine in the way that Haworth Parsonage has become,

77

nor Micklewike the tourist attraction that Haworth is." He rubbed his hands. "And a very good thing too, many will say!"

That gave Charlie to think, and he thought about it during the other early speeches. So Mr Suzman did not expect the farm to become a shrine, if he was to be believed. His mind was not on large sums of tourist money from entrance fees, from postcards or tasteful souvenirs (replicas of Joshua's axe, perhaps?). What then was behind this? Where was the scam?

Charlie surfaced again during the speech of a lady who remembered Susannah Sneddon being pointed out to her in the main street of Batley Bridge when she (the speaker) was a girl of three — "And six months later she was dead." Next came a lady who said she'd discovered the novels of Susannah in ancient, unused copies in the Halifax Public Library in the 'fifties, and therefore claimed some sort of superiority over those who had only cottoned on to her since the feminist revival of interest in the books. Soon a gentleman was making a plea for Joshua's novels which managed to make them sound totally unreadable. Charlie began to divide the speakers in his own mind into those who simply wanted to declare some kind of witness and those who were making a bid to get elected to the Committee. But all of them were staking claims, whether large or small, in the Sneddons, their books, their lives and their fate. Each of them swooped down and bore off their gobbets of flesh.

He perked up when arrangements for the afternoon were announced. There were to be tours of the farm arranged at twenty-minute intervals, so that there were never to be more than ten in the house at any one time. This was "to preserve the intimacy and privacy of the atmosphere there, the feeling that this was a place where *writers* worked," as Mr Suzman put it. Mrs Cardew, the lady taking minutes, would be at the door at meeting's end, registering everyone into a conducted tour at their preferred time in the afternoon if that was practicable. Mr Suzman hoped that would help to break the ice, as would the party in the farmhouse in the evening (admission three pounds, with wine and cheese served, and some tickets still available). As the session began to break up Charlie came up behind Lettie Farraday, who had sat silent during the meeting, apparently not craving any brief moment of limelight by revealing her connection with the Sneddons. In her, it seemed, the predatory instinct was weak.

"Enjoy it?" he asked.

"A real hoot," she said, with a touch of sourness. "When are you going on this tour?"

Charlie shrugged.

"Whenever. Say two, just after lunch? Do you want the support of my strong right arm?"

"It would be welcome to get up there, Dexter. But don't let me cramp your style."

When they had registered for the two o'clock tour and emerged into sunlight now stronger and warmer, Charlie said:

"Talking about my style, I've got a date at the Black Horse. Coming?"

"To the Black Horse, yes. To play gooseberry, no. You had more than enough of me yesterday."

"Have you rung the Home yet?"

Lettie grimaced.

"I got the number from Enquiries. I tried to ring after breakfast, but nobody was answering. Probably busy spooning porridge down the old people's throats."

"You've not softened at the prospect?"

"I have *not!* But I'm still torn two ways: downright hostility to the idea on the one hand, and greedy curiosity on the other. Neither of them very attractive emotions . . . There was a pay phone at the Black Horse, wasn't there?"

"Yes. In the little hallway near the loos.

As private as you can expect in a country pub." They had come through the maze of uneven back streets and stood surveying the place, now thronged with casual drinkers standing outside in the sun with jackets and cardigans over their arms. "Especially on a day like this."

"I'll cope," said Lettie, tottering through the entrance. "Is your date here?"

Charlie peered through the haze of the Saloon Bar.

"She is. And her father came too."

"Eventide Home. Can I help you?"

The voice was strong and sensible sounding. Lettie took heart.

"I hope so. My name is Lettie Farraday. I believe you have a . . . a patient there called Martha Blatchley."

"Yes, we do."

"Well, I'm . . . this is difficult . . . I'm her daughter."

There was a stunned silence.

"Oh."

"Precisely. I went to America long ago . . . before the war . . . and we haven't kept in touch. To tell you the truth it's a shock to find she's still alive."

"I suppose so."

"It's difficult to know what to do. I needn't

say that we weren't close. Frankly, we didn't get on."

"I can understand that."

"Is she still . . . is she still in control of her faculties?"

"Yes. I think I can say she is that."

"Ah . . . But if that's the case, I don't know that she'd welcome a visit from me. I don't suppose you'd have any idea whether she would?"

"I can't really say. Generally speaking the old people here regard having children, and children who visit, as a bit of a status symbol. On the other hand, your mother . . ."

"Yes?"

"Well, she doesn't always think the same way as the others. Doesn't usually, to tell you the truth. And I have to say I've never heard her mention you with affection."

"I'll bet you haven't!"

"On the other hand that doesn't mean she wouldn't welcome a visit. The days are long, and she doesn't watch television like the others do."

"Oh, she doesn't doesn't she?"

"Says it's a matter of principle."

"I thought it would be something like that. A matter of cantankerousness, more like."

"Well . . . I could mention that you're in the area and see what the reaction is. We wouldn't want a scene, of course."

"You wouldn't get one. I can rein in *my* cantankerousness, I promise you that."

"I'm sure you can. Well, shall I do that? And where could I contact you?"

"Maybe it's best if I ring you this evening. Will you still be on duty?"

"I will. Ask for Mrs Clandon, will you? Because there are one or two others on the staff who — "

"Yes?"

"Well, frankly, they practically refuse to have anything to do with your mother."

"Oh my! Am I looking forward to this meeting!"

And her mother came too. Too.

Holed over by the wall was the girl Charlie had his date with, intimidatingly fenced in by the figures of her father and mother, who seemed to be acting as some kind of familial Praetorian guard. They were all holding glasses, so Charlie elbowed his way to the bar, bought himself a pint, and then went over.

"Hi," he said.

The girl brightened immediately.

"Oh hi. Mother, father, this is — "

"Charlie Peace," said Charlie, holding out his hand. It was taken reluctantly by the father, hardly more warmly by the mother, who seemed always to take the lead from her husband. Rupert Coggenhoe was posed to present a leonine profile to the common herd, but his eyes glowered with a quite naked suspicion.

"You know my daughter?"

"That's right. How did you think this morning went?"

"Oh, you were at the meeting?"

"Yes. I thought your contribution was very interesting. It was good to hear the viewpoint of a present-day writer."

God damn me for a liar, he thought. There was an infinitesimal thawing in both of the pair.

"I did try to use that perspective to put over thoughts that might not otherwise get an airing. You think I made my point?"

"Oh, absolutely."

"How did you and my daughter get acquainted?"

"We met up at the farm yesterday and got talking."

"Talking? What about?"

My God! thought Charlie. This sort of inquisition would probably be inadmissible under the Police and Criminal Evidence Act.

"Oh, the Sneddons, what else?"

"You're interested in their books?"

"Of course. That's why I'm here. In their books and their lives."

"Which books have you read?"

"Daddy!"

"I'm in the middle of *The Black Byre*. I've read *Orchard's End* and *The Barren Fields*. But as I say I find their lives fascinating too."

"What aspects of their lives?"

Charlie would like to have conveyed to the girl that if she would plead a visit to the loo he would pretend to get himself another drink and they could both disappear somewhere. But he couldn't think of any delicate pantomime to suggest this, and in any case the fiercely inquisitorial paternal eyes were fixed upon him.

"Oh, how all this creative power seems to have sprung from such a deprived background. And of course their deaths."

"Oh?"

"We were discussing the deaths yesterday and wondering — "

"Do you think I might interrupt?"

That blessed American accent! It was Lettie, riding to his rescue as a return for his favours of the previous day.

"I was very interested in what you were saying about your own books, and in particular — what was its name? — *Starveacre*?"

85

"*Starveacre*, yes." He said it loudly.

"I wonder now, what name did you say you used in writing that book? And would it be currently available in the States?"

She had his complete attention. The girl, perhaps quick from long experience, murmured something about the loo, while Charlie drained his glass and said he could just about manage another. In minutes they were back in the main street and heading for one of the few places where they might reasonably hope to be alone on that particular day — the scruffy back lane by which Charlie had first come into Micklewike.

"Now you know why I sometimes feel like Elizabeth Barrett Browning," said the girl bitterly. She jumped up to sit on a stone wall and Charlie lounged alongside her.

"I think it might be an idea if you told me your name," he said.

Chapter 6

A Tour of the Shrine

It was, it turned out, Felicity, and in the course of the next hour or so they learned a good deal more about each other than their names. Charlie liked what he learned, though he was bewildered by the sort of control her parents seemed to exercise over her. He resisted the impulse to probe, however: there had been girls in his life who had complained that he couldn't stop being a policeman. Even without probing, though, Charlie received the impression that Rupert Coggenhoe was a tiny talent with a monster-sized ego — and a burden of grievances against a world which did not accord him the recognition which he thought was his due. Exploration of this topic left them no time to go into Charlie's background, which was exactly what he intended.

When they got back to the Black Horse

at about a quarter to two he braved the lowering looks of her parents with an insouciant wave and gave his arm to Lettie Farraday for the walk up to the farm. She took it demurely.

"Thanks for the rescue," he said. "I hope you didn't have to endure him all through lunch?"

"I managed to edge away when they started getting worried about their missing chick," she said. "On the grounds that I'd 'taken up too much of his valuable time.' Before that I had to endure a lot of horse manure on the subject of 'the writer's craft.' "

"The man's a bore."

"And a petty tyrant. Watch out for him."

"I'm not poised to propose marriage to the girl," Charlie pointed out. "Want to stop for a rest?"

"No. I'm getting used to this street. Again."

Around the gate to High Maddox Farm a little knot of people were gathering, with others strolling further along the road and stopping to get a view of the farm from a different angle. Mrs Cardew, the lady who had taken their names at the meeting, was installing herself beside the gate, and as they approached she began with a tight smile to let the tour people on her list through the gate, waving them unnecessarily in the direction of the farm. Among the group Charlie registered what he (like Mr Suzman) had already put down as the Scandinavian couple, and Gillian Parkin, from the evening before. Otherwise there was a motley collection of elderly couples, the odd young enthusiast, and one Japanese woman, birdlike and eager. As they straggled towards the farm's main door their hands were shaken by Gerald Suzman, who introduced them to an ample, motherly woman.

"Mrs Marsden, our excellent curator."

Mrs Marsden was friendly and welcoming. When she registered from Lettie's "Hello" that she was American she shot her a glance, but she merely said: "It's good to know that Susannah Sneddon is being read in America."

"To a degree," said Lettie cautiously. "To a degree. You'll know about the article in *Time* magazine, I guess."

"Yes. Mr Suzman was delighted with that."

Now the group was assembled, and Mrs Marsden smiled and ushered them through into the farmhouse. In spite of the sunny day outside the interior was dim. Charlie realized that, as with many old rural buildings, the windows were too small for such a large room. Not much reading done in such buildings in former centuries, he concluded. He blinked, and stood for a moment close by the door to get accustomed to the poor light.

"I'm here to answer questions, if I can," said Mrs Marsden. "If anyone wants information or explanations, just come along to me."

"You go round at your pace, Dexter," whispered Lettie Farraday to Charlie. "And I'll go round at mine."

Which Charlie interpreted quite rightly as a wish to be on her own.

He sauntered round, his eyes beginning to be accustomed to the gloom. As furniture and other objects came to be seen more clearly the impression started to form of something decidedly artificial. It was all superficially accurate, but dead, like those fake streets of Victorian shops that some museums have: altogether too posed and pristine to present any real feeling of the visitor having strayed into another century or another way of life. On a rough wooden table in the kitchen area of the barn-like room there was a rolling-pin, a floury surface and an appearance of pastry being made: only he knew that if he touched it, it would not turn out to be pastry. Nor would the fire in the range turn out to be a real fire, so that the kettle on the hob beside it would never boil. There was not enough dirt, not enough muddle. The floors should be gritty and muddy, not swept clean.

As the thought struck him his eye was caught by something. He squatted down on his haunches. If all around was vaguely bogus, here was reality! Charlie knew a bloodstain when he saw one, though he did not recall seeing one as old as this. Was it here that? —

There were legs standing beside him, and looking up he saw the curator — Mrs Marsden, was it? — looking down at him.

"Sorry," he said, raising himself upright. "Morbid. I suppose you were hoping nobody was going to notice that."

She smiled tolerantly.

"We always knew there would be some as would ask. Now you've noticed it, you'll have been seen noticing it, so everyone will, and tell people in the other groups who come in later. It's natural, all part of the story — the sad part."

"So that is — "

"Oh yes. That's where she was found. Fallen by a chair just like this one here, that she'd been sitting on. Well, not so much fallen as felled. He came up from behind. They say in the village that's one thing he didn't botch up. They say it must have been a quick death."

91

"He'd have been used to killing animals, I suppose."

"Oh yes, he'd have done that."

Charlie nodded his thanks and moved on. His eyes were now fully accustomed to the lack of light. He saw Lettie standing stiffly by a small table with a typewriter and piles of paper beside it, her forehead furrowed. She stood there for some time, then moved painfully on towards the old sofa under the small window that admitted the sun so begrudgingly. Charlie moved towards the table himself, but the Japanese lady was there before him, peering at the little framed card on the wall beside it.

"Ah! Susannah Sneddon's lighting desk!" she said, looking enthusiastically at Charlie.

It was indeed, or something that could stand in for it. The typewriter was an ancient machine, a real bonecruncher, that looked as if it would require special finger-strengthening exercises to operate with comfort. There were pencils, a stubby fountain pen and a bottle of Waterman's blue-black ink. The pile of typescript was on thin paper, brown with age and curling at the edges, though lower down the pile, apparently, the pages became photocopies. Peering close with the Japanese lady Charlie recognized a torrid love scene from Susannah's best-known novel.

"Ah — *The Barren Fields!*" the lady said, pleased with herself for recognizing it.

Charlie nodded. He thought to himself that this, the little table and all the apparatus of writing, seemed the most authentic things — or at least the most convincing things — he had seen so far. Perhaps this was because Susannah Sneddon, whatever her merits, was undoubtedly a writer. She was never more than marginally a housewife. He longed to type "The quick brown fox jumped over the lazy dog" on her machine, but he caught Gerald Suzman's eye on him, and he smiled and desisted. "There's a quick brown fox" he thought to himself, with reference to Gerald Suzman. Charlie knew quite a lot more about Mr Suzman than anyone else in the room.

Gradually the tour party was moving towards the stairs and up to the first floor. Charlie moved over to Lettie and offered her his arm, and she gratefully accepted it. The stairs were wooden, rickety and uncarpeted.

"Beastly things!" said Lettie.

They separated when they got to the top. Charlie thought that the bedrooms had more of a "feel" to them than the big room downstairs. Perhaps this was because there was less need to suggest a multiplicity of activities. They were there to be slept in, and that was that: there were heavy blankets, coarse sheets, and rough bedside tables with books turned down on them: in Joshua's bedroom the book was *Dubliners*, in Susannah's a May Sinclair. There was a third bedroom even more sparsely furnished than the other two. That seemed right: the Sneddons were not people who had visitors. There was a bathroom, the plumbing of which, the visitors were informed on an information card, was a later addition, circa 1950. It was hoped to restore it to roughly what it had been in the Sneddons' time. The lavatory was an addition too, formed from part of the spare bedroom, but there was no intention of restoring things to what they were. Charlie Peace, a real townee, shuddered to think what the arrangements were before it had been put in.

From the window of Joshua Sneddon's bedroom he saw the next tour group beginning to assemble at the gate by the road. He noticed that Randolph Sneddon was among them, and was shaking the odd hand — awkwardly enough, but at least showing willing. On the landing Lettie Farraday was ready to go downstairs, and he gave her his arm.

She was, he noticed, unusually silent. At the bottom of the stairs Mrs Marsden was directing people towards the back door and they thanked her with a smile. The door was in the kitchen area, latched, but with two new and heavy bolts fitted. It creaked, dramatically and convincingly. Outside they were suddenly transported to suburbia, finding a small but colourful garden, with flagged paths and a riot of Spring shrubs and bulbs making a brave show against the wuthering climate of Micklewike.

"All wrong," whispered Lettie to Charlie. "She only had a few primroses out here."

The whisper — there were two other couples from the tour already in the garden — confirmed what Charlie had begun to suspect. When they had wandered through the paths and reached the little patch of lawn beyond the flowerbeds, he said:

"You've been keeping quiet about your connections with the Sneddons. Don't you want it known?"

"It is known. It'll be all around the village, since Milly Winkworth recognized me. And that rather over-enthusiastic student last night may well have told people, unless she has some idea of keeping me to herself. But I don't want to be badgered by Gerald Suzman, don't want to be made part of his set-up, at least not yet. I may decide to say something tomorrow, but it will be in my own time."

They wandered round to the front of the farm, where Gerald Suzman was once again holding court for the next tour. He was being cornered, however, by Gillian Parkin and the Scandinavian girl, who, having interests in common, had clearly teamed up.

"I assure you a transcript is already being prepared," he was saying, smiling ingratiatingly. "The new edition of *The Barren Fields* is already at the publishers, and we hope to have a full text of the first two novels ready for publication by the end of the year."

The Scandinavian woman's boyfriend was standing a bit aside, and he raised his eyebrows at Charlie.

"Vi are a bit out of things here," he said. "Textual problems in the Sneddon novels — not my scene!"

He was a strong-boned man in his mid-forties, with the flesh of good living beginning to cling. He had a coarse fair beard, but the hair on his head was thin. He was looking with tolerance at the trio nearby: Gillian Parkin and her friend shoulder to shoulder, Gerald Suzman fending them off — and the women knowing they were being fended off, but unable to do anything about it. Bent forward, eager, there was something in their stance of the beast of prey. But Gerald Suzman did not look like anybody's prey.

"I can't say I'm much bothered by little changes in the texts," agreed Charlie easily.

"A bit difficult to see Susannah Sneddon as a Shakespeare," commented Lettie dryly, "with scholars arguing over emendations. I think I'll creep away. That young lady is a bit too inclined to regard me as valuable source material!"

Charlie was about to move away with her towards the road when he saw that there was another couple waiting impatiently beside the little group, obviously hoping to talk to Gerald Suzman. The man was tall, gangling, with a craggy, misshapen face and hideous teeth which obtruded themselves on the observer by their fang-like shape and discoloured state. His wife was small and dumpy, with a puddingy face and faded hair that she let fall around in an apparently random manner. After a moment or two Gerald Suzman saw them and used them to make his escape.

"Someone else wants to talk to me. I'm quite happy to discuss the manuscripts *any time,*" he said in parting — Charlie thought with particular emphasis to the Scandinavian woman, indeed with a look at her that was almost meaningful. "Yes?" he said, turning towards the couple. "Did you want to see me?"

The lanky man bent over him. Charlie moved closer.

"My name is Felix Potter-Hodge."

"Oh yes?"

"My grandmother was a great friend of Susannah Sneddon's."

"Really?"

Now Mr Suzman's interest was genuinely aroused. His body took on a new spryness, tense with interest. He gave them his real as opposed to his token attention.

"How did they know each other? Was it a literary friendship?"

"Oh no. They were at school together, first here in Micklewike, then in Batley Bridge."

"How fascinating. A Micklewike girl, then. And did your grandmother talk much about her friend?"

"She did occasionally, yes. But she married young and moved to Ilkley, so her memories were mostly of their schooldays."

"They could be very valuable. We have very few records of that time."

"She never wrote anything down, of course."

"I imagine not. If only the revival of interest had come earlier . . ."

"But there are letters!"

"Letters? They corresponded?"

"Oh yes. Not frequently, but regularly, over a long period. It was a case of maybe two or three letters a year."

"And you said — did you say 'there *are* letters'?"

"Oh yes. She kept them all."

"She'll be dead by now, of course."

"Yes, she died in 1960. But we inherited them."

"Really?"

"Well, we inherited the house. The letters were in an old suitcase in the attic. We might well have thrown them out, but we'd heard her talk of her friend the novelist, and we thought she wouldn't want them destroyed. So we just left them up there."

"They're still there?"

"Actually we brought them down when there began to be all this talk about Susannah Sneddon. Dusted them off, you know, and read a page or two."

"Their place is here!" said Gerald Suzman, emphatically and enthusiastically.

The man's craggy face crumbled into a smile. His place in the Susannah Sneddon story had been acknowledged. His part of her was being exhibited in the light of day.

"We would be quite happy to lend one or two letters for exhibition," he said.

"No, no: they should all be here. As an archive. There are very few letters of the Sneddons in existence that we know of. They didn't have a great many friends. The letters should be here — I would be happy to make you an offer for them."

The man turned his stubbled, cavernous face to his wife's.

"Oh, I don't think we'd want that, would we, Mavis?"

"Oh *no*," she said, surprisingly positive. "No, we didn't think of *selling*."

"But why not? Susannah Sneddon was nothing special to you."

"Well, but she is now," said Felix Potter-Hodge, nodding complacently. "We've never had anyone of interest in our family. My grandmother was just an ordinary farm girl from around here — Janet Hodge, who married an Ilkley grocer older than herself. Mind you, I daresay she was a very intelligent woman, for someone with very little education. Anyway, now we have someone not *in* but at least connected with the family who is of interest, and we'd like to hold on to what we have of hers. Of course if anyone

wants to study the letters, or see the snapshots — "

"Snapshots?"

"There's one or two, in with the letters.
As I say, we'd be happy to make them all
available to people. People like those two
young ladies you've been talking to, people
with a special interest in Susannah Sneddon.
But we'd want to hold on to them ourselves,
wouldn't we, Mavis?"

"Oh, we would. Definitely."

The little knot of visitors was getting res-
tive. The star performer was being mon-
opolized. Gerald Suzman looked around, and
began to usher them towards the door and
Mrs Marsden.

"We'll talk about this," he called, in the
direction of the Potter-Hodges. "We certainly must talk about this."

Charlie watched the little group go towards the farm, meet Mrs Marsden, and
then pass through into the gloom of the
farmhouse, Felix Potter-Hodge having to
bend his ungainly height to get in the low
door. Charlie had a slight, unaccountable
sense of unease. Shaking himself he turned
away and began walking, deep in thought,
to the gate. There he found Lettie Farraday
watching him through narrowed eyes. He
hauled himself out of his reverie.

"Sorry," he said. "Dreaming. Where to now?"

"Down, I hope, to my waiting taxi."

They began the walk down the main street.

"Your fame doesn't seem to have spread yet," said Charlie. "No Sneddon fans crowding round you with questions about the home life of Susannah and Joshua."

"No," said Lettie briefly. She looked round to see if they were out of earshot of the woman on the gate. "I'm the one with questions."

"Oh?"

"Let's start with one to you: what exactly are you here for, Dexter?"

Chapter 7

Mother
and Daughter

"Eventide Home."

"Oh hi. That is Mrs Clandon, isn't it? This is Lettie Farraday again."

"Oh, good evening, Mrs Farraday. By the way, it is Mrs *Farraday*, isn't it?"

"Yes."

"Only your mother has been . . . well, *going on*, frankly, about your being married to a foreigner — 'an ovsky or a chinsky' were her exact words."

"Ciesinski. My first."

"Oh, I see. I should have guessed. Only I'm afraid your mother said she wasn't going to have you bringing any 'ovsky or chinsky' in tow."

"No danger of that. Ciesinski died at Okinawa, two years after we were divorced. Howard Farraday died of a stroke six years ago."

"I don't suppose she would have objected to a Farraday."

"She would. He was American."

"Ah yes. Well, in spite of all this, I don't get the idea that your mother is opposed to your visiting her."

"Oh."

"Quite the contrary, really. I get the impression that she's almost pleased at the idea. As close as she can get to pleased."

"You surprise me."

"Maybe stimulated would be a better word than pleased."

"That sounds more likely. Anticipating trouble."

"She does very much enjoy trouble, doesn't she?"

"Always has."

"Of course the question is, what is she looking forward to doing or saying? Any nastiness is usually of her making, and you mustn't think she is likely to make it easy for you."

"You don't have to tell me. I know my mother."

"Yes, of course, but you see . . . a lot of time has passed since you knew her."

"Too right. I get you. People don't improve with age. I know I don't."

"She is . . . well, she's quite inventive in

the things she thinks up to annoy people, or make them feel small."

"I get your message loud and clear. I'll take it that she's now even more damned difficult than she used to be. When do you think would be a suitable time for me to come?"

"Whenever you like. She has no better times."

"What about this evening? Get it over with."

"That would be fine. Let me see: they're having their meal now. We settle them down around nine o'clock. Any time before about eight, then?"

"I'll get on to my tame taxi driver. I'll be with you in half an hour, at most three quarters."

"Splendid. I'll prepare your mother . . . No, on second thoughts perhaps I won't. She tends to save up wounding things to say."

"She'll have prepared those already. Oh my! I'm sure looking forward to this!"

"Mike?"

"Charlie! Where are you? Can we talk?"

"A phone booth in Batley Bridge. Don't be so cloak-and-dagger. I haven't seen anything that calls for George Smiley tactics so far."

"Everything clean and shining and above-board?"

"Well, I don't know that I'd quite say that. But everything to the contrary is really just a *feeling,* based on what I was told at Scotland Yard about the man, not on anything that's happened since I've been here."

"You mean because he isn't straight this can't be straight?"

"Precisely, which is why I'm here, isn't it?"

Charlie had phoned Mike Oddie, his superior in Leeds, from Scotland Yard on Thursday. There he had been briefed on the series of forgeries and literary con jobs that seemed — very tortuously, as a rule — to lead back to Gerald Suzman. It had been a fascinating collection, not least because of the interesting ways Suzman had of distancing himself from the transactions. Charlie's old friend Superintendent Trethowan, going through the catalogue with him and sharing his delight at the man's inventiveness, said that the interesting thing about the Micklewike Weekend was that, at last, the man was putting himself in the centre of the picture.

"My bet is," Charlie now went on, "that, whatever he's up to, it's going to emerge slowly — maybe over the years. Certainly so far I haven't the foggiest what he's going to come up with."

"Nothing remotely suspicious?"

"No. People keep appearing out of the woodwork and making contact with him: people who knew the Sneddons, have mementoes of them, research students and people like that. You might say everyone wants to stake a claim: they're sort of hovering over Micklewike like a flock of vultures. But nothing that I've heard so far gives me a clue to what his particular pound of flesh may be. Oh, by the way — "

"Yes?"

"You remember I said I'd stand out like a sore thumb here, and you said that one thing no one would suspect me of being was a policeman?"

"Yes."

"I think you were wrong."

"Someone's on to you?"

"An American lady. British-born American. Black policemen are very common in New York."

"Damn. I suppose I should have thought of that. There were bound to be Americans there. Have you told her anything?"

"No. I just said there were reasons for my being here that didn't demand devotion to Susannah Sneddon's great novels, but that

I couldn't discuss them."

"Did she accept that?"

"Well, on the surface, yes. But I think it's bound to alert her to Gerald Suzman and his activities, if she wasn't already. She's very nice, and I suppose she could even be useful. She knew Susannah Sneddon."

"Old, then."

"Oh yes."

"I don't know that Susannah Sneddon has anything to do with what our man is up to."

"The fact is, Mike, we haven't the faintest notion of what our man is up to."

"True. What are your plans?"

"Tonight there's a party. Wine and cheese, would you believe?"

"For a very junior detective constable you do have it cushy."

"Give me an acid house party raid any day."

The Eventide Home was a substantial stone house on the outskirts of the village of Hipperholt, built for one of the local notables, and now housing a collection of forgottens. It took mostly old people whose fees were paid by the National Health, but it tended them in a perfectly humane way, which was not the case with all such establishments.

108

Dorothy Clandon would not have worked there if it had been otherwise. Lettie, hobbling in on the arm of her taxi driver, liked her at once: sturdy, sympathetic and — the prime quality necessary — patient.

"I'd like you to wait for me, please," she told the driver. "This may not take much time at all."

"Look, I'll go and have a chat with old Stan Richards. Used to live down the road from me. You take as long as you like — or make it as short as you like."

He winked at her and took himself off. Lettie turned to Mrs Clandon, sighing.

"Well, we'd better get it over with."

"Right . . . I should warn you that your mother is likely to make a wounding remark as soon as she sees you. It's a habit she has. She's probably thought up several possibilities."

"Yes, I remember she always liked to take people down right from the start."

"That doesn't mean things will get any better later on, though they might, depending on her mood."

"You really don't have to warn me," said Lettie grimly. "My expectations are at zero. And remember I can walk out whenever I want, so I have the advantage on her. I didn't have that option as a child."

"Well . . ." said Mrs Clandon, smiling bravely. "Here goes."

She led the way to a small room off from the far end of the hall, a warm, cosy room which she often used for encounters that might prove difficult. Lettie followed slowly behind her, and her heart thumped as she pushed open the door. Don't be a fool! she told herself. What can she do to you now?

She turned into the doorway and found herself regarded by a pair of malevolent black eyes in a wizened frame. It was the smallness of her mother that struck her first: it wasn't how she remembered her. She had shrivelled away to a hideous ragbag of skin and bone: her hands on the chair arms were like skeleton hands, carelessly covered over with what looked like stray bits of discoloured skin already in the process of decomposition. The face was baggy and sagging, like a motley array of purses and shopping bags. Only the eyes were truly alive — and the voice, as Lettie immediately found out.

"Well, you do look a sight!" her mother said, in a rasping contralto.

The wine and cheese evening was held in the farmhouse itself. It was lucky that the weather had stayed fine, otherwise Charlie calculated that some of the guests would have been forced on to the stairs or the landing. There were something like fifty people present, and by now the processes of getting to know, getting to like and getting to avoid were well advanced. One no longer needed an excuse for talking to anybody. In addition, one could wander round the house and the garden at greater leisure than in the afternoon. Charlie wondered that Mr Suzman was not more worried about things being stolen, but as he strolled around himself he realized that a great many — in fact most — of the objects were "typical" ones, things that would have been found in farmhouses of the time, rather than actual relics of Susannah and Joshua Sneddon.

"I bet the Sneddons didn't throw many parties like this," he said to the Scandinavian pair, both clutching glasses of white wine.

"If they vere the cocktail party types, vi vouldn't read them," said the man.

"Why do you read them?"

"Because they — no, because *Susannah* is werry much back to the soil, back to the dark core — you say that? — to the dark core of our life. Like our Knut Hamsun in Norvay. I'm Vidkun Mjølhus, by the vay, and this is Vibeke Nordli."

"Is that why you read her?" asked Charlie, turning to Vibeke. She nodded briskly.

She seemed a brisk, no-nonsense person.

"In a way. But with more of a feminist slant. She's very good on women's sexuality, on women's right to a sensual life of her own. Carries on from Charlotte Brontë in a way. I want to translate some more of the books into Norwegian, once there's a proper text established in English."

"Is there some problem with the text?"

"Of course there is. It's been censored — cut and changed, watered down. Susannah was a woman, wasn't she? Women weren't *allowed* to say the sort of things Susannah wanted to say."

"I believe D. H. Lawrence had the same problem," murmured Charlie. He wanted, on the strength of having read *Sons and Lovers* for Advanced Level, to add "And he was a hell of a lot better writer," but he decided not to. Hardly appropriate for a founder member of the Sneddon Fellowship. And not sensible to arouse hostility. He was reinforced in that feeling by being the recipient of a decidedly hostile look a moment later. The Coggenhoes were as usual crowding round their daughter, giving her no space to be herself, and Rupert Coggenhoe, who directed the glare at Charlie, was telling him he was not forgiven for the morning's exploit. Charlie shot him one of his most dazzling and guileless smiles, a shameless exhibition of incisors and premolars. Then he moved to behind the man's back, from where he mouthed the word "After" at Felicity. When she nodded, her father's shoulders shot round suspiciously, but by then he had only a view of Charlie's back.

Charlie was, he found, by the little table with the typewriter and pages of typescript that he'd inspected that morning. He looked back at the text now with more time to look closely. It was, as he and the Japanese lady had recognised, the steamy scene in the loft of the barn from *The Barren Fields*, but as he read in detail he realized that the scene was even steamier than he remembered:

She felt his hard chest against her breasts, his scalding breath on her cheeks, and as she whispered her compliance she felt his harsh, calloused hands on her thighs, then between her legs, and as she parted them willingly, urgently . . .

"Gosh!" Charlie raised his eyebrows. He'd check with his copy in the b. and b. later (if he could stand the excitement) but he was willing to bet that the published version was considerably toned down and shortened. Cunning old Gerald Suzman! Not only to put a page from one of Susannah's hottest scenes at the top of the pile, but one that had been censored, presumably by her publishers. What it showed bore out Vibeke Nordli's contention: Susannah had wanted to be considerably more explicit than she had been allowed to be. How many had noticed this, he wondered? It amounted to a promise of heady delights to come when the full texts were published.

Charlie moved lithely through the throng, down to the kitchen area and out the latched door to the garden. Ten or twelve guests, singly or in couples, were enjoying the rich evening sunlight.

"She must have loved her garden," he heard one middle-aged lady say to a similar friend. "I can just imagine her looking for the daffodils poking their heads through the winter earth, or lovingly tending those roses and azaleas."

Yuk!

"Actually she only had primroses here," he said as he passed.

It was a mistake. The ladies turned on him accusingly.

"How do you know?"

"An old lady told me. Someone who knew

them, used to come here when they lived here."

"Who's that then?"

I really got myself into this, Charlie thought. He reined himself in. Lettie had told him she wanted to lie doggo for the moment.

"I'm not sure I should say. I ought to respect her privacy. But she's here for the Weekend. Maybe she'll say something at the meeting tomorrow."

They looked hard at him as he made his escape. Clearly they were putting him down as a bullshit artist. He walked with what dignity he could muster over to the lawn, where Randolph Sneddon was holding court with the sort of slightly forced bonhomie that Charlie had reluctantly admired earlier in the day.

"I'm afraid I don't know anything about the texts," he was saying. "I hate to admit it, but I only started reading the books recently."

"So you don't have any say over who edits the new editions?" Gillian Parkin demanded, a terrier expression on her face, her manner positively inquisitorial. Vibeke Nordli was beside her, and they made a formidable duo.

"None at all. Nor any interest, I'm afraid."

"You can't insist that we *see* the manuscripts?"

"Oh, you'll have to talk to Mr Suzman about that."

"So you didn't inherit them?" Vibeke Nordli asked.

"Oh no. They come from the publishers, I think."

"What did you inherit? Any of the things here?"

"I'm afraid not. I didn't have anything at all to offer Mr Suzman. What happened was, when they died, or soon after, the farm and all its contents were put on the market. Public auction — quite a few sensation seekers there, I wouldn't mind betting, buying up mementoes of a minor local scandal. So I know Mr Suzman's hoping that more things will turn up . . ."

"But didn't your people care *anything* about her? — "

"Country people are very unsentimental, you know. And I believe my grandfather was rather straight-laced."

Over her head Charlie and Randolph Sneddon looked at each other, two tall men communing. Sneddon's face was a picture of wry long-suffering. Charlie was interested to register that now, apparently, he was accepted by the other as one of his part of the human race.

"Now, now, Mrs Blatchley," began Mrs Clandon.

"Don't you 'Now-now' me like I was a school-child! I'll tell my own daughter she looks a sight if I want to!"

"You don't look any oil painting yourself," said Lettie equably.

"Don't talk to me about painting! What have you plastered your face with?"

"It's called makeup." Lettie sat down heavily in the other chair. "People have been painting themselves since prehistoric times. You don't have to stay, Mrs Clandon. Mother and I will get on just fine."

Dorothy Clandon looked dubious for a moment, then nodded and withdrew.

"Well!" said her mother with relish as the door shut. "I never expected my daughter to come home a painted woman!"

"I should think that's exactly what you did expect," said Lettie. "Make-up may not make me look any better, but it makes me feel a hell of a lot better."

"Language!"

"Well, I think we've exhausted that topic. How have you been all these years, Mother? When did Father die?"

The lips parted in a sort of snarl, revealing

a small and miscellaneous collection of discoloured teeth.

"Nineteen sixty. Or it may have been nineteen seventy. I don't remember exactly. Time doesn't mean much any more. He'd been ill for years. He was terrible when he was poorly, always whining and complaining."

"It must have been a bundle of laughs in the old house. You were still in the cottage in Tanner's Alley, were you?"

"All the time. Right up to when I had to come here. The Methodist minister was on at me for years to come here. Said I shouldn't be living down there in Micklewike all on my own. Very concerned he was."

Lettie's opinion of the cunning of Methodist ministers took an upward turn. She had no doubt of his real reason for thinking her mother should leave Micklewike for the Eventide Home.

"And what did Father die of?"

"Pneumonia in the end. Just like your brother Paul." She nodded meaningfully. "He was a good son. If only Paul had lived. He'd have taken care of me."

Lettie saw that her dead brother was now shrouded in an affection and regard that had never been lavished on him while he lived. She knew her brother would have got away as she had. They had often discussed it, in

118

bed at night. It had given an added sad pang to his early death.

"And what have you lived off? Do you get some kind of pension?"

"Of course. It's more than enough. There's plenty as complain, but they're the soft livers. I've never been one for the vanities of life."

"Except the vanity of a thoroughly good opinion of yourself," Lettie opined.

"Those that walk in the way of the Lord shall see the Lord plain," her mother said complacently. Lettie smiled. Her mother had not lost her habit of producing improvised scripture, then.

"I've no doubt you're right," she said. "And before very long, too. I suppose you're wondering why I've come back?"

This was greeted with a hard stare.

"Why should I wonder that? There's no explanation needed when someone comes home to see their mother."

My God — she's more deluded than I thought, Lettie said to herself. She carefully ignored the suggestion.

"There's this conference, you see. You may have heard of it. A sort of weekend in honour of the Sneddons."

"What?"

"Don't you remember, Mother? The Sneddons, Joshua and Susannah? You used to go and work for them at High Maddox Farm."

"Oh, I remember *them*. Why would anyone honour *them*? I shouldn't have demeaned myself, going up there. She wrote mucky books. All novels are lies, and she wrote dirty lies."

"Well, it's a point of view, I suppose. I used to go up with you sometimes, didn't I?"

The lips parted again into that wolfish snarl.

"Thought herself such a Lady Muck, didn't she? Couldn't even keep the place clean. Couldn't keep herself clean either, for all the money she earned with that filth."

"The farm is a sort of museum now."

"A what?"

"A museum. A sort of shrine to the Sneddons."

"Shrine! That's blasphemy, that is! But then, there's nowt so daft as folks."

"Do you remember going up there sometimes when Susannah Sneddon was writing?"

" 'Course I do. Used to shoo me off somewhere so she could get on wi' writing her mucky lies."

Lettie bent forward and asked her mother a question. When she got her answer she was satisfied that, as with many old people, her memory for things that happened long ago was better than her memory of recent events. She almost felt glad she had come.

Chapter 8

Coming Out

On the Sunday morning Charlie awoke with feelings of dissatisfaction: what had he done, found out, achieved? He had attended the inaugural meeting of a literary society that was, to all appearances, completely aboveboard, composed of genuine enthusiasts as well as others with connections, close or peripheral, to the Sneddons, their writings, and their tragedy. He had seen things, heard things, that interested him, but nothing that had got him any further forward. He had also, be it said, had a rather enjoyable couple of hours with Felicity Coggenhoe after the wine and cheese party, but that could hardly be said to have contributed to his investigations — apart, perhaps, from some grisly details that filled in the picture of the awfulness of her parents.

Perhaps it was just because he felt he had

got nowhere that he decided to stay over that night.

"I'd like to do a bit of walking this evening," he told his landlady when she brought in a laden plate that included black pudding and practically everything else that conceivably could be fried. "And perhaps some more tomorrow before I go back to Leeds."

"I'll keep the room for you," Mrs Ludlum said comfortably. "No probs, as they say in *Neighbours*."

Charlie shuddered quietly to himself and got down to making a dent in the pile in front of him.

When he had finished, or eaten as much as the human stomach could bear, he went to his room and dressed rather more sportily than he had the day before. When he was ready, on an impulse, he sat down at his typewriter and wrote "Manuscripts? Where? Where from?" Then he left the house on the Haworth Road and walked down to Batley Bridge. He didn't, though, start at once up the hill path to Micklewike. Instead he went to the Duke of Cumberland and, using the phone in the foyer, rang up to Room Twenty-one and Lettie Farraday.

"My, you are attentive!" she said.

"Attentive — and curious."

"Well, you don't have to tell an old woman

that a young man who's attentive has an ulterior motive."

"Are you going to the meeting?"

"Sure. But I need a quarter of an hour or so to turn myself into what my mother would call a painted woman. Are you walking up, Dexter?"

"I made a resolution to walk up every day, to compensate for all the stodge I'm eating."

"Have you ever yet made a resolution you haven't broken?"

"Never."

"Come up in the taxi with me then."

"You're on."

"Wait down there and I'll see you in fifteen minutes."

Once she was settled in the back of the taxi Charlie got in beside her and asked:

"Well, how was your mother?"

"A vicious old crone with a veneer of religion."

"Did you row?"

"Nothing we couldn't both handle. I managed to stand her for nearly an hour."

"What did you talk about?"

"Never you mind, young man. You're a good deal too curious for someone who won't tell me *why* he's curious." She thought for a moment and then asked: "Dexter, has it occurred to you that there's really not much of the Sneddons at High Maddox Farm?"

Charlie nodded.

"Yes, it has. Oddly enough not when I went around for the first time, but when I was there at the party last night. It's all 'typical' rather than actually things of theirs. 'Their bedrooms must have looked rather like this,' rather than 'This is Susannah's bed, this is her bedside table.' Most of it could have been picked up for a song — probably was. But I can see the difficulties, and I suppose he's hoping that genuine stuff will turn up."

"Hmmm. I may say I recognised nothing from my visits as a child. To me it was more like a stage set than a museum. What is he getting out of it, do you suppose?"

"Search me. He's not going to make a fortune from admission charges. It's hardly Haworth, as he said yesterday. I imagine the farm was probably going cheap, with agriculture in the state it's in at the moment, but still . . ."

"But still, indeed. I take it he sees it as the shrine of a new cult. But a very minor one, surely. I just don't see what's in it for *him*, Dexter."

"Nor," said Charlie grimly, "do I."

"And we're agreed there must be something, aren't we?"

"It seems likely," said Charlie, more guardedly.

"That's what you're here for, isn't it?"

"No comment, as politicians ought to say when people make allegations about their sex life."

Lettie got out a note to pay the taxi driver, and looked meaningfully at the man, who was now a friend.

"And you haven't heard a word of this conversation, Len."

"I haven't. Any more than I heard any of the names you called your mother on the way back last night."

"Too right. I'm glad we see eye to eye."

The crowd milling around the village hall was much more animated and united than it had been the first morning. As Charlie helped Lettie out of the taxi he saw the two ladies who had been making sentimental remarks about Susannah Sneddon, the devoted gardener and flower-lover. He whispered to Lettie:

"Are you 'coming out' today?"

"What can you mean?"

"As someone who knew the Sneddons?"

"I was thinking of saying something at the meeting."

"Good. You could become the Fellowship's

mascot. Or perhaps its bête noir. Anyway, there are these people I want you to meet." And leading her over to the sentimental pair, he introduced her: "Ladies, this is Lettie Farraday, from New York. I mentioned her to you yesterday: born and brought up here in Micklewike. She used to go up with her mother to clean for Susannah Sneddon."

He saw the suspicion in their eyes change to greedy interest: they were in the presence of one who had touched greatness. He thought he heard the flapping of large wings. He stood there for only a second or two, but even so the questions had begun tumbling out: "Did you really? What was she like? What was her relationship with her brother really like? Did they row?" As he moved away he thought to himself that he would rather like to know the answer to that last question. And as he surveyed the smiling, chattering throng, and saw several members of the new Fellowship dart over and join in the inquisition of Lettie, a further thought occurred to him. Lettie was 'coming out' today, but effectively as far as the village was concerned she had been 'out' since Friday evening. Mr Suzman had close contacts with the village: he had been frequently in the area while setting up the Museum — that much Charlie had been told at Scotland

Yard. So someone from the village, probably Mrs Marsden or Mrs Cardew, the woman who was acting as Secretary, must surely have told him that at the Weekend there was a woman who had known Susannah Sneddon, had known the interior of the farm while she lived there. Yet he had made no attempt to contact Lettie.

Odd.

He moved over to the group around Gerald Suzman, which consisted mostly of the Coggenhoe family. He braved the looks of hostility from the great author and his wife and grinned at Felicity — a grin that expressed appreciation of their time together the previous evening. Then he stood listening. It was Mr Suzman who was doing most of the talking.

"Yes, indeed, a *very* busy weekend. But exhilarating too! Glad when it's over? Not at all, dear lady. But perhaps a little relieved that it's all gone so well. I shall relax tonight in my cottage in Oxenthorpe with a bottle of my favourite Alsace, and perhaps soothe myself with Mozart's last and greatest opera."

"The Magic Flute?" hazarded Mary Coggenhoe.

"No, no, dear lady: *La Clemenza di Tito.*"

Phoney! thought Charlie, moving away. He didn't know much about Mozart's operas, but he did know that his greatest was not one nobody had heard of. Still, the phoniness of Mr Gerald Suzman was not in doubt: the question was what particular piece of trompe l'oeil he was fabricating here in Micklewike.

Charlie led the drift back into the hall, and once again took his place towards the back. The opening part of the meeting was mainly formal: the Fellowship was set up, an interim constitution was established, and an Executive Council voted into being. Mr Suzman proposed a lean, active Council of five members, to get the Fellowship off the ground. He put forward five names, and these were agreed from the floor: Rupert Coggenhoe seemed to be there to represent Literature; Randolph Sneddon was there to represent Family; Gillian Parkin was there to represent Academic Research; the lady who acted as Secretary, Mrs Cardew, was there to represent Micklewike; and Mr Suzman was there as the Founding Father.

Things got more interesting when they came to Any Other Business. Mr Suzman had said at the beginning of the meeting that he hoped this would become a general discussion of the experience of the Weekend, what members hoped for from the Fellowship, suggestions for next year's gathering, and so on. Rupert Coggenhoe said he thought walks to places featured in the Sneddon novels would be an appropriate and enjoyable feature for future weekends, and mentioned Beckett's Falls, which had featured so prominently in *The Hard Furrow*, and which, coincidentally, could be paralleled with a waterfall in his own novel *Starveacre*. One of the sentimental ladies suggested a church service on the Sunday morning of the Weekend, and Gillian Parkin protested against the emasculation ("significantly there is no female equivalent of that term") of Susannah Sneddon's texts in their printed versions. Vibeke Nordli called for the establishment of international Chapters of the Fellowship.

It was quite late in the meeting when Lettie Farraday got up to speak.

"Mr Chairman, I wonder if I can say a few words as one who knew the Sneddons." (Small buzz of interest, turning heads. Mr Suzman nodded, as if this was something he'd known all along, perhaps had arranged.) "Though you wouldn't think it from the sound of me, I was born and brought up a few hundred yards from this hall. My mother used to go up and clean for the Sneddons once a week, and sometimes in the school holidays I used to go up with her. Of course what you've got up there now is a sanitised version of the farm. I'm not criticising you for that: nobody wants to go into a mess of dirt and disorder. But that's what it was. If they hadn't employed my mother it would have been a slum. Thinking back on it, I can respect Susannah for that: she made her choice, and the choice was that she wanted to be a writer. So far as she was concerned the rest could go hang, and it did. But that wasn't how we saw it in the village at the time."

"I'm sure it wasn't," said Mr Suzman, apparently just to say something.

"No, to us she was a mucky housewife, a real sloven. And that was a real *judgment* on somebody, for us, then. And I think you should try to get *something* of that into the Museum, because that was a distinctive part of Susannah Sneddon's life: dirt, poor food badly cooked, nasty smells. Another thing: the farmhouse is far too full of things from the 'twenties — fire-tongs, pudding basins, beds, knives and forks. But the Sneddons never bought anything. The things the farm was full of were much older — 'nineties stuff, I suppose, or even earlier. So the fire-tongs and the cutlery and the kitchen utensils would have been Victorian ones, heavier, uglier — and dirtier, of course."

"That's something I hadn't thought of," interjected Mr Suzman. "It shows how very little Susannah thought of her immediate physical surroundings."

"That's right. She didn't care about them at all. What they did with their money — whether it went to subsidize the farm, or was saved up, or what — I don't know. But it didn't go on clothes, it didn't go on furniture or food or everyday comforts. Susannah — and Joshua, but I only had much to do with Susannah — she just lived for her writing. And by the way, she only ever wrote by hand. That typewriter for Susannah is out of place: Joshua used one, but she never did. Got someone to type her things up for the publishers, I suppose, but she used an old fountain pen — you got that right, I think, in the one up there — and wrote the novels in ruled exercise books. I'm pretty sure Joshua never typed for her: what little time he had he used for his own books. And of course it was said in the village that he resented hers. By the way, someone mentioned a church service. Neither of them *ever* went to church. Joshua used to say in the pub that he'd done his last praying in the trenches in 1915 . . . Oh, one last thing: don't ever do away with that loo. There's some things we do a hell of a lot better today."

Lettie sat down to laughter, a little smattering of applause, and a great deal of interest. The meeting meandered towards its close, and when it was finally over, with happy admonitions from Mr Suzman to be sure to come back next year, there was a minor rush of people, both pushy and shy, over towards Lettie to question her.

Mr Suzman, Charlie noticed, did not join the rush. He talked earnestly to the new Secretary to the Fellowship, Mrs Cardew, and gradually one or two members of the newly elected Council went over to them, and they all began taking out diaries and arranging dates for meetings. The last Charlie saw of Suzman was his standing by the door and announcing that he was going to drive away and have a nice *quiet* lunch on his own before the final event, the afternoon lecture.

"I believe the Chinese in Batley Bridge is very good," ventured Mrs Cardew. "Though it was closed down briefly by the health people a little while ago."

"I would *never* go to a restaurant that was given a clean bill by the health inspectors," said Mr Suzman grandly. "They would obviously have their priorities wrong."

Charlie waited outside the hall, talking in a desultory way to Vidkun Mjølhus. The man had an amiable impenetrability to which

Charlie couldn't relate. Susannah Sneddon might have described his eyes as bottomless pools, but what was in their depths? Ageless wisdom, or simply nothing? After several minutes' conversation which blandly skimmed surfaces Charlie saw Lettie emerge from the hall, surrounded by an admiring troupe. He could see that she didn't need his help to the Black Horse, and when the Coggenhoes came out he muttered apologies to the Norwegian and went over to them.

"Yes?" said Rupert Coggenhoe, as if he were a doorstep salesman.

"There's a farmhouse restaurant a mile along the road to Abbothall," said Charlie, with his most ingratiating smile. "Felicity and I were thinking of giving it a try for lunch."

The hostility of the Coggenhoes prevented them seeing the look of surprise, pleased surprise, on their daughter's face.

"That's quite impossible," said her father. "As you will know, I have just been elected to the Council. I need to be in Micklewike to be available to members."

"Oh, absolutely," said Charlie. "We quite understand. Come on, Felicity."

"Felicity! You can't think of . . . Felicity! We've hardly seen anything of you!"

But they were talking to her back.

"Hardly seen anything of me!" grumbled Felicity, as they walked at a pace that verged on running. "How can they say that when I've seen a great deal of them?"

The lady who ran the farmhouse restaurant, an attempt to fight the agricultural depression, clearly regarded them as an odd couple, but she had had several other customers who were attending the Sneddon Weekend, so she took them in her stride.

"It's the murder that attracts you," she said, half-accusing, half-amused. "If it weren't for that, you'd not be here. Morbid, I call it. Now, I've got a lovely hot-pot . . ."

The walk there and back took them a while, because they weren't hurrying, and by the time they got back to Micklewike the lecture had started. Charlie wasn't too disappointed. It was on "Susannah Sneddon — a Marxist Perspective," given by a lecturer from Bradford University. Charlie wondered how much longer there would be Marxists to have a perspective. He and Felicity mooched around Micklewike, noticing the other conferees who were giving the lecture a miss. These included the unattractive pair who had inherited letters from Susannah. Charlie watched curiously their progress around the town. The news had got about, so that other members of the Fellowship

135

kept coming up to them and asking about the connection. The unattractive pair blossomed unattractively.

About three they went back to the village hall and mingled with the audience coming out as if they'd been there all along.

"I'd better stay with the oldies for the rest of the day," said Felicity. "You've got my phone number."

"Right," said Charlie. "I'll be around here, and at the Duke of Cumberland keeping an eye on Lettie."

Felicity raised her eyebrows.

"What do you mean? Why do you have to keep an eye on her?"

"Oh — just if she needs my help getting anywhere," said Charlie.

But it was not just physical assistance that Charlie had in mind. There niggled in the back of his brain the thought that Gerald Suzman's reaction to Lettie's presence had been odd. Of course there were no doubt others in Micklewike who had known the Sneddons . . . Yet Lettie's particular connection to the farm through her mother — wouldn't one have expected that Suzman would welcome her with open arms, question her, consult her?

As ordinary members were questioning her and consulting her. Charlie had little need to worry about her for the rest of the day. Her taxi driver took her down to the Duke of Cumberland, where she sat through the late afternoon and early evening, pausing only for a brief dinner, surrounded by loyal Sneddon admirers, racking her brains for memories that would answer their queries. There could be no danger there . . . Yet *danger,* oddly, was what preoccupied Charlie, and he hung around, occasionally catching Lettie's eye and communicating twinkles of amusement. At last she was tired and ready for an early bed. Charlie stood up, ready to attend her. Felicity, ensconced with her parents in a cosy corner nook, saw him resume duty as Lettie's attendant and suddenly realized that, though he had told her a great deal about himself, none of it was recent. What was he actually doing in Leeds? Her parents had been very insistent in their questions about what he did, and all she could give them was the description that he had given her: security and investigative work. Her father had immediately decided he was part of a criminal gang — one of the rare signs he gave of a creative imagination. But Felicity's brow creased. Exactly what sort of work was he in?

As Charlie and Lettie hobbled through the bar and out to the foyer, Charlie thought he had better find out Lettie's plans.

"How long are you going to be here?" he asked.

"Oh, till Tuesday, I suppose. Or Wednesday. I may go up and see Mother again. Oh, don't smile. There's a sort of . . . grisly fascination about it all."

They started up the stairs.

"What sort of lock is there on your door here?" Charlie asked.

"Oh, just an ordinary Yale lock."

"Any chain on the inside?"

"Yes, there is a chain."

"Put it on, will you?"

"Why?"

"And maybe put a chair against the door and keep the phone close."

"Why?"

"Let's just say: better safe than sorry. Do it, Lettie."

"I suppose you're the guy who knows."

He waited in the corridor till he had heard the chain being put up, and a chair being drawn across the floor. Then he shook himself, dissatisfied, went down the stairs and then out into the twilight.

Chapter 9

Corpse

Charlie was coming down to breakfast next morning when the phone in the hallway rang. His landlady was bustling through from the kitchen with a laden tray, and Charlie took it from her and went into the dining room. He had asked for scrambled eggs, as a light option, but his heart sank as he saw it was surrounded by substantial mounds of fried bacon, mushrooms and tomatoes. He was just setting the things out and mentally saluting the pile when he heard Mrs Ludlum say:

"Oh yes, he's just down. He'll be tucking into his breakfast. Won't it wait? It'd be a pity to — oh, urgent, is it? Who shall I say, then?"

Charlie was already at the dining room door, and she handed him the phone.

"It's a Mr Oddie."

She stood in the hall, lingering in the doorway to the dining room.

"Mike?"

"Charlie, I want you to get a taxi. Have you got the number of the local people?"

"Yes — what is it? Not Lettie Farraday?"

"No the man himself. He's got — he had — a cottage called Moor View, just outside Oxenthorpe. I'd pick you up, only it's too far out of my way."

"Dead, I take it?"

"As the proverbial dodo."

Charlie pressed down the telephone rest and then dialled the Batley Bridge taxi firm.

"I want a cab right away, to 40 Haworth Road. The name is Peace. To Oxenthorpe."

Mrs Ludlum shook her head, grief-stricken, when he dashed back into the dining room.

"Surely you can make a start on it?"

"No way. You have it."

"Oh, I don't eat stuff like that."

"Well, I'll tell you what" — he took up the bacon and put it between two slices of toast — "emergency rations. Could you find me a bag for this?"

As she came back with it he was at the front door and his taxi was drawing up. He had grabbed his wallet, and he handed her the cost of his room for three nights.

"Here's what I owe you. If you could

keep the room for me tonight, just in case. I'll ring you later."

"But what is it? What's the rush?"

"Murder."

"Murder? Who's been murdered? And what's it to do with you?"

"Can't say. It'll be on the local news. I should have told you I'm a policeman."

And leaving her open-mouthed in the doorway (to ring around to her friends, to mention Oxenthorpe, and to start making all sorts of connections, many of them surprisingly accurate) he climbed into the car. The taxi driver was not Lettie's friend, but he had observed the scene in the doorway.

"Not often we get a fare to Oxenthorpe," he angled delicately as he pulled away from the kerb.

"It's a rush job. I'm a policeman," said Charlie, to foreshorten the process.

"Must be a rush job if they can't send a police car for you . . . And something pretty important."

"Suspected murder or manslaughter."

"Really. . . ? That Gerald Suzman has a cottage over Oxenthorpe way."

"It's his cottage we're going to."

"Is it him as has been murdered?"

"Don't know yet, do we? Till he's been identified."

"Oh, right . . ."

"Why did you mention him?"

"Don't know. It was the name that sprang to mind. He's had a pretty high profile round here this last weekend."

"What did people here think of him?"

"Oh, he was perfectly nice to people, no question of that. But they couldn't . . . well, let's just say they didn't think he was in this just for love of Susannah Sneddon and her novels. But they couldn't see what there was in it for him."

"They're not alone," said Charlie, in heartfelt tones.

As the car sped through moorland and grazing pastures Charlie meditated on his feeling that all the people at the Weekend were, in their various ways, laying claim to a stake in Susannah Sneddon. And the biggest stake of all was that claimed by Gerald Suzman. Yet the lesser claims all seemed obvious enough: knowledge of the woman, inherited letters from her, genuine love of her books. It was only the largest claim that was mysterious. No doubt Gerald Suzman had a love of the books . . . Charlie pulled himself up at that thought. That wasn't really the case: there was plenty of doubt. Gerald Suzman saw primarily in the books some . . . some future possibility, some prospect of profit,

142

some glittering financial prize. His connections with literature were strong, but their foundations were not laid in love, but in money.

"Any idea where the cottage is?" the taxi driver asked.

"None. It's called Moor View, and it's on the outskirts. We can ask the locals if necessary. News is bound to have got around."

But it was not necessary to ask. Gerald Suzman's cottage, conveniently for him, was on the Batley Bridge side of Oxenthorpe. It was up a wide lane off from the main road into the village, and it marked itself off by the number of police cars outside it. They pulled off the road, Charlie paid off the driver and got a receipt. Then he went to make one more policeman.

The cottage had a small, ill-kept garden at the front, and an iron fence separating it from the lane. Charlie stood at the gate to get a view of it before he went in. It was a genuine cottage — a rural worker's home when it was built. It was small, poky and ill-lit, but it had the advantage of being sturdy and belonging to the landscape. No attempts had been made at prettification beyond a clematis, an old, straggly plant, which grew by and around the front door. The other honest thing about the little building was its name: it did indeed have a view of the moors — a particularly fine one if you averted your eyes from the road to the left and took in rolling acres of rough scrubland to the right.

Charlie swallowed hard before knocking at the door: he had not yet got used to dead bodies, though in honesty he had to admit to himself that a degree of hardening had taken place — becoming habituated did lessen the shock.

The door was opened to him cautiously, and he saw at once why: the body of Gerald Suzman was just inside the door, and all the business of measuring and photographing was having to take place in difficult, cramped circumstances. With due precaution he stepped around the body and looked. It was a hideous sight. Mr Suzman had been battered to death.

"Who found him?" he asked one of the Keighley policemen standing in the background.

"A neighbour. The postman tried to deliver a parcel, got no answer, so he left it at the house down the road. The woman there had a key, because this bloke's not often here. It's more of a holiday home than a residence."

"Yes, I know."

"Do you know him?"

"Yes. Or mainly *of* him."

144

"Looks a respectable bloke enough."

"So did Lord Lucan."

The doctor came over, and they exchanged the greeting of men slightly known to each other.

"Oddie's coming, I hear."

"Yes. Should be here any minute."

"I'll tell you what I know, then, or what I guess, and you can pass it on. As you can see he was battered with something — *what* I can't guess as yet."

"Any sort of struggle?"

"No, not struggle, but he knew what was happening, wasn't caught unawares. I'd guess at an initial blow to the forehead, then, when he was staggering, a further series of blows from behind."

"A lot of strength needed?"

"Some. But that's a dodgy matter, difficult to judge, as you know very well. I'm not going to rule out a woman, just to make your job easier. Time? Well, I'd guess late at night, and I'm not just going by the fact that he was wearing his dressing-gown. He looks like the kind of chap who could be wearing his dressing-gown any time of day."

"I think he probably was. More the dressing-gown than the track suit and trainer type, anyway."

Ten minutes later, when Charlie's favourite

superior, Superintendent Oddie had arrived, and the crowd in the little living room was beginning to disperse, the two of them were able to pause for a moment and look down on the disfigured body.

"Difficult to say," said Mike Oddie, "whether he had just answered the door, was trying to escape through it, or just happened to be near it."

"The doc doesn't think he was caught unawares," said Charlie, and gave Oddie a summary of what he had said.

"That seems to agree with the look of the thing," said Oddie, nodding. "But even if he had just answered the door there'd be that moment of awareness, when he saw the man — the visitor — raising the weapon."

"The doc isn't committing himself on the sex of the killer."

"Quite right too . . ." Mike Oddie averted his eyes from the body and looked around the room. "Comfortable enough, but hardly lived in, would you say?"

Their eyes raked round the drab living room, which the little hallway opened into. Clearly it had once been two rooms of roughly equal size, but some time ago it had been made into a good-sized living room with a small kitchen opening off from it. It was decorated drably, with a fawn wallpaper that was in places dirty and starting to peel. There was evidence, where the paper was darker, of other furniture having stood there. Mr Suzman had clearly bought the property, made it marginally his, but had not thought it worthwhile to stamp his own fairly distinctive personality on to it. The furniture was standard, either second-hand or surplus to requirements in his other home. The only indications of taste were in the books and the records.

"I wonder when he bought it," mused Mike Oddie. "Was it just acquired for the Sneddon festivities? A short-term home for a short-term project, perhaps?"

"Oxenthorpe is pretty convenient for Haworth too — much closer, in fact," Charlie reminded him. "Remember that highly suspicious business of the Brontë manuscripts?"

"Yes. That was twenty-odd years ago, though. I've made enquiries about that at the Parsonage. There seems to have been a whole lot of dodgy business in the past, the pretty distant past, that they're still very cagey about. But the general view there seems to be that, just because of those dodgy deals, some of them involving Thomas J. Wise, the forger, most collectors would be much better informed these days. Quite simply, they're more suspicious."

"I bet there are collectors who *want* to believe they've got genuine Charlotte Brontë stuff," commented Charlie.

"Agreed. There's no fool like a man with an obsession." Mike Oddie went over to the smart compact disc player in the wall unit. "Well, he was listening to the Bruch violin concerto."

"Ah — not *La Clemenza di Tito*?"

"Eh?"

Charlie reported the conversation with the Coggenhoes, imitating Suzman's stance and voice, with its mixture of the pompous and the epicene.

"You should have been on television," said Mike appreciatively. "I get the impression of a pseud — is that right?"

"Pretty much so."

"Well, I suppose that's no great surprise."

"I'm not sure that he went down altogether well with most of the people at the Weekend. With a few exceptions they were ordinary, enthusiastic readers who just happened to have a particular love of the Sneddons. He gave the impression of being very much the sophisticated Londoner, whereas most of the rank-and-file people at the Weekend were provincial, particularly Northerners."

"Maybe his manner was one that went down well with collectors, but wasn't well adapted to the real literary enthusiast."

"Maybe. I've never met a collector."

"Me too neither."

They peered down at the assortment of records and books neatly arranged in different parts of the unit.

"Romantic concertos mostly: Grieg, Tchaikovsky, Dvorák. What you might call the Everyman kind of classical music."

"Not the impression he tried to give. But the books are a bit different," said Charlie, crouching to look along the spines. "Limited choice. All the Susannah Sneddon novels, of course, in the Untamed Shrew paperback edition. A bit of Brontë, lots of D. H. Lawrence in several different editions — who'd want two or three copies of *Women in Love* in their holiday cottage? Oh, and some Joyce. But what he was actually reading was *Brideshead Revisited*."

"A different sort of lush read," said Oddie, "and probably more to his taste than the Susannah Sneddon novels." He looked at the book, turned face down on the shelf closest to one of the armchairs.

"That suggests he hadn't yet gone to bed."

"That doesn't tell us much about the time of his death," Charlie pointed out. "We don't know anything about his habits. Shall we take a look upstairs?"

149

But upstairs told them even less. It was, even more than the ground floor, a camping-place rather than a home. The bed had not been slept in, the drawers contained silk pyjamas and a range of fairly natty shirts, the suits in the wardrobe were Savile Row, and the man had shaved with a heavy, expensive safety razor and used a strong aftershave.

"Nothing of interest here," said Oddie. "Now, I think we'd better alert people in Batley Bridge, to try and stop people who were there for the Weekend leaving, or at least make sure they leave addresses."

"We can't insist, can we? We have no proof the murder is connected with the Weekend."

"No. But if they hear it's murder, and someone they know, a lot of them will stay. Who do you think we should contact?"

"The Black Horse in Micklewike, the Duke of Cumberland in Batley Bridge, and the Tourist Office there," said Charlie. "I've got all their numbers. Oh, and there's a woman in Micklewike who's Secretary of the Sneddon Fellowship. Mrs Cardew I think the name is. I don't have a number for her, but she'll certainly have an address list of members."

"Right. Could you contact anyone you can? We can use the phone downstairs now. I'll have a last look round, then we'll go and talk to the woman who found him."

The woman was Mrs Tuckett, and she lived in a decent, uninspired 'thirties detached house directly on the main road into Oxenthorpe, with a bed and breakfast sign in the front window. She was not to be drawn on the subject of Mr Suzman, because she said she simply did not know him.

"I'd just go and clean there now and then, when he was going to come up, and he paid me generously because I had the key, and looked after the place when he let it out, that kind of thing. But I didn't *know* him at all. Perfectly friendly, quite the gentleman, but that's as much as I can say."

"It must have been a shock finding him."

"It *was!* Horrible! Because I saw him only last night — full of life he was then."

"You saw him last night? What time was that?"

"Early on. About seven. He wasn't in his dressing-gown then. I knew he was off back to London today — would have been, had he lived — and I went to see if he wanted anything doing while he was away. There was music going, a symphony or something of that sort, and I had to bang on the door to be heard. Anyway, he and this other chap were having a drink."

151

"Other chap? You didn't know his name?"

"Oh no, I'd never seen him before. Young-ish chap. Dark. Very good looking."

"Could be Randolph Sneddon," murmured Charlie to Oddie.

"Anyway, Mr Suzman said he wouldn't be coming up till he had some kind of Committee meeting for this Fellowship thing. Said he'd give me a call before then. The young man said it was time for him to be off, and he walked with me down to the road where he'd left his car."

"Didn't say anything to the purpose?"

"Just wasn't it nice the evenings were drawing out."

"What kind of car did he have?"

"Oh, I don't know anything about cars. One of those sporty jobs. Dark green."

"And there is nothing else you can tell us?"

"Not really . . ." She turned aside to the hall table and took up a substantial package. "There's this parcel. When I found him there I just ran back here to phone the police. Who should have it, do you reckon?"

Mike Oddie peered at the package.

" 'Bennett and Morley. Publishers.' " It was a soft, flexible package. "Some kind of proofs, maybe. Don't suppose they're important. As to who should have them, I suppose eventually his heirs, whoever they are. We'll take it now."

"I know he was never married," said Mrs Tuckett. "That much he did tell me of his private life. 'Too fly to get caught, dear lady' was how he put it."

"Maybe," said Mike Oddie, as they walked back to the car, "we shouldn't be concentrating too much on the people at the Conference. Maybe we should be asking *'cui bono'?"*

"And what does that mean?" asked Charlie.

"It means 'Who gets his hands on the loot?' "

"I always heard that Latin was an economical language."

"It is. *Multum in parvo.* 'A lot in a little.' "

"It's like being sidekick to Lord Peter Wimsey," Charlie complained.

Chapter 10

Questions (I)

They sat for some minutes in the car, waiting for a policeman to arrive from Keighley to guard the cottage. The question they mulled over was where to start — and more specifically where to base the first stages of the investigation. The body was here in Oxenthorpe, the Weekend had been in Micklewike, and many of the people they wanted to talk to were in Batley Bridge. In the end the last seemed the most convenient centre: Mike Oddie drove himself and Charlie to Batley Bridge to set up a temporary incident centre in three vacant rooms at the Duke of Cumberland. Then he handed Charlie the key to the car, telling him to go and try to catch any remaining conferees in Micklewike.

"We want statements from any and all of them," he insisted. "Ask them to come down here and tell us anything they know before they take off. And that Secretary woman, and the caretaker: they may know a lot more about Gerald Suzman than the conference-goers. I'll tell this Mrs Farraday that we want to talk to her, and the Sneddon character if he's still staying here, but I won't do any actual questioning until you get back."

At the Black Horse Charlie found the land-lord pottering around somewhat lethargically after the busiest weekend of his tenancy.

"Still here? Oh, there's that girl — what's her name? — Parkin. She's here till Friday. And those two from Sweden or Norway or wherever it is. What do you want them for?"

"I'm police. There's been a murder."

"Oh yes?" The man's sluggishness seemed endemic. He was apparently unsurprised that the young man who had drunk in his pub over the weekend and mingled with the Weekenders should turn out to be a police-man with a murder on his hands.

"You don't know where they are, these three?"

"No idea."

"Will you tell them the police want to talk to them?"

"Aye, I'll do that if I remember."

Charlie got out before he lost patience. He had a quick dash around Micklewike and up to the farm. There he had his only stroke of luck. He saw wandering round in the vicinity of the farmhouse Vibeke Nordli, apparently on her way back from the spinney. He stood at the gate and hailed her.

"I wanted to see it — experience it — when there was nobody around," she said as he approached. "Magic!"

The rapture seemed genuine. She struck Charlie as much more open, more candid than her boyfriend or husband. Then he remembered that feeling he had of flapping wings when she and Gillian Parkin got on to the subject of the manuscripts.

"Sounds like you haven't heard the news," he said. "Suzman's been murdered."

That really stopped her in her tracks.

"No! You can't be serious!" She looked at him with distress on her face. "But what's going to happen? What about the Fellowship? And the new edition of the novels?"

Charlie kept his eyebrows unraised with difficulty.

"Well, that's not really our first concern," he said. "I'm a policeman, by the way. We want anyone who was at the Weekend to come down to Batley Bridge and make a statement. Do you know where Gillian Parkin is?"

"No, but I'm meeting her for lunch. Down in Batley Bridge."

"Well, if you'd both come along to the Duke of Cumberland some time this afternoon we'd be grateful. What about Mr — Herr I can't pronounce his name — "

"Vidkun. Vidkun Mjølhus. He was at breakfast. I don't think he's leaving till tomorrow."

This time Charlie's eyebrows did rise. She looked at the puzzlement in his face and laughed.

"Did you think we were — like — together? Partners? I'd never met him before last Friday. We went around together because we are both Norwegians."

"Sorry. I got the wrong end of the stick."

"I come from Tromsø, he comes from Oslo. About as far apart as London and Inverness, I should think. Further."

"You're an academic, aren't you? Is he too?"

"No. I believe he has a bookshop — *antikvariat*, what's that? antiquarian bookshop, somewhere in Oslo. If I see him I'll tell him you want to talk to him."

"And do you know where the Secretary lady lives? Mrs Cardew?"

"Yes, I'll come and show you."

Mrs Brenda Cardew lived in one of the smaller cottages on the main street, round the corner from where Lettie Farraday had grown up. When she opened the door her eyes were red from weeping.

"I'm sorry. I can't do any Fellowship work today. I've just heard — "

Charlie flashed his ID at her.

"I'm a policeman."

"A policeman!" She had gulped back her tears and now stared at him. When she spoke there was a note of outrage in her voice:

"But you were at the Weekend!"

"That's right. I'm also a policeman."

"But *why* were you at the Weekend?"

"We can go into that later. I can see you've heard of Mr Suzman's death. We wanted to talk to you because you must have known him better than most of us who just came for the Weekend."

"I'm sure I didn't. Not on a *personal* level at all."

"A lot of people wondered why he was setting up the Fellowship, whether there was anything behind it."

"They did, did they?" Crossness made her flush. "People have such nasty minds. The Fellowship was set up by a few dedicated and hardworking people who gave a lot of their time without reward because they're *devoted* to the memory of Susannah Sneddon and to her novels. Mr Suzman was the most dedicated of all."

"Ah," said Charlie, with the inscrutability of a civil servant. "Now, I wonder if you have a membership list . . ."

Charlie got from her a copy of the complete list of those who had signed up for membership during the Weekend. He also got a promise that she, and Mrs Marsden the curator if she was available, would come down to the Duke of Cumberland during the afternoon to make statements.

Down at the Cumberland the police were in the process of taking over part of the pub — a takeover that Mike Oddie told the landlord would probably be brief. The landlord looked as if he hoped it would be long-lasting: the tourist season wouldn't perk up until June, and the police would pay him. He was pretty sure they would attract sensation-seekers too. Charlie found Oddie in the foyer and brought him up to date with what he'd done in Micklewike. As they were talking he suddenly realized that they were being watched from the door into the public bar. On Rupert and Mary Coggenhoe's faces there was a struggle between the hostility that hitherto had been automatic and a dawning realization that they'd got something wrong. Charlie was no accomplished lipreader, but then he didn't need to be to catch what the great writer's wife said to the great writer.

"I think he must be a po*lice*man!"

When he detached himself from Oddie and went to fetch something from the car outside they accosted him by the door, now with an uncertainty that landed them somewhere between the reproachful and the ingratiating.

"You didn't tell us you were a policeman."

"You didn't seem interested in my career or prospects."

"Yes, well, I think we may have . . . made a bit of a mistake." In so far as one could shuffle standing still, Rupert Coggenhoe shuffled. "I gather we're all to be questioned."

"That's right. Are you wanting to get away? Would you like to go first?"

"Well, we're booked in till tomorrow. But there are things I'd like to be doing — in connection with the Fellowship. It seems natural that I should — well — "

"Take over?"

"Take the lead, after Mr Suzman's unfortunate death . . . Er, I take it you *were* at the Weekend as an enthusiast for the Sneddon novels?"

Charlie smiled non-committally.

"I'm very interested in the murder-suicide

160

as well," he said. "As I think I told you. Questions later, and in the other direction."

"Oh yes . . . Yes, I suppose so. But you're not assuming, are you, that this has anything to do with the Fellowship? There must be lots of other possibilities."

"Oh yes, we'll be following up lots of other lines of enquiry," agreed Charlie. "*Cui bono*, for example. Now, if you'll excuse me . . ."

When he came back into the foyer from fetching his papers from the car the Coggenhoes had disappeared, but Lettie was making her way painfully downstairs. He darted to help.

"Ah . . . always there when needed. Well, I can't say that it's all *that* much of a surprise that you are a policeman, Dexter. I gather we're all to be interviewed?"

"That's right. Do you want to 'go on' early?"

"Not particularly. I've got all the time in the world, and I'll enjoy watching the other suspects."

"Do that, please, Lettie, and listen too. Your lack of mobility means you can stick around without arousing questions. When are you leaving?"

"When you do, or when this is over. You don't think I'm going to pass up the chance of being close to a murder investigation, do you? I'll dine out on this for the rest of my life!"

"Will you be going up to see your mother again?"

"May do . . . The shrinks would have a name for me, wouldn't they?"

"Delay it as long as you can, will you? We may have a question or two for you to put to her."

"You don't think this has anything to do with the Sneddons, do you?"

"As I've just told the Coggenhoes, all avenues will be explored."

"You've got the jargon too," said Lettie admiringly. "My, I'm enjoying myself!"

When Charlie settled down with Mike Oddie in one of the three bedrooms they had taken over (in the other two were policemen, local and from Halifax, taking calls from the public and doing what they could by phone to illuminate the life and background of Mr Gerald Suzman), Oddie shoved a paper across the table to Charlie.

"These are the conference-goers who are still here."

"Right . . . Some of the names I recognise, some — "

"Most of them will only be able to tell us things that you will know already."

162

"You don't need to tell me that police work is ninety per cent tedium."

"Randolph Sneddon went off very early this morning — he'd told the landlord that's what he'd be doing. I've been thinking: you said there was this couple who had a bundle of letters from Susannah Sneddon. That's exactly the kind of thing Gerald Suzman would be interested in."

"Oh, he was. I've got an idea they drove over, rather than stayed in the area, but that's just an impression. I've got the complete membership list here . . . Double-barrelled name . . . Here we are: Potter-Hodge, Felix and Mavis. An address in Ilkley. I seem to remember he said his grandmother moved there."

"Well, we'll want to talk to them when we've interviewed the people here. Shall we get going now?"

When later, very much later, Charlie was back in his room at the bed and breakfast, with a half bottle of red wine that the landlord of the Duke of Cumberland had been very reluctant to accept money for, so thronged had been his bars all day with the curious, the professionally interested and the frankly ghoulish, he went over all those interviews, and eventually typed up anything he thought of interest, anything he might want to think over in any spare time he might grab during the investigation. The highlights were regrettably few and far between. Most of the people had seen what he had seen, heard what he had heard, and no more. Few had plucked up the courage to talk to Mr Suzman, and those who had could recall only banalities and pieties. Suzman had been, to the enthusiasts, a disappointment. Some had talked to the Potter-Hodges, and had come away rather shocked that they hadn't bothered to read most of the letters. There were some, of course, who were anxious to play down their involvement with Gerald Suzman. Rupert Coggenhoe was one such.

"Never spoke to the man before Friday," he insisted, sitting tensely in the chair, bent forward.

"How did you get to know about the Weekend?"

"There was a piece — rather a snide piece — about it in the Books supplement of the *Sunday Times*. Made a rather silly comparison between Suzman's Dolphin Square address and the subject-matter of *The Barren Fields*. I just looked him up in the telephone directory and wrote expressing interest. That was early on. Later there was much more publicity, pieces in the colour supplements

— that kind of thing. He was good at getting the right kind of publicity."

"Had you heard of him before?"

"Name rang a bell — no more than that. Friend told me he was some kind of specialist antiquarian dealer."

"And your conversations with him over the Weekend?"

"Purely utilitarian. Dates for the new committee to meet — that kind of thing."

"So you have no strong impression of him as a person?"

"No *strong* impression . . ." Coggenhoe considered. "Not really the sort of person I'd associate with Susannah Sneddon's novels . . . Too smooth, plausible . . . More like a politician, really."

When he had gone to "set about getting the Fellowship back on an even keel," Charlie said:

"If it's him it won't have anything to do with the Fellowship."

"Too keen to draw attention to it, you mean? True. And murder to gain control of a literary society doesn't seem all that likely."

"Oh, I don't know," said Charlie. "Lettie says that everyone who goes in for beanos of that sort is ever so slightly mad."

The interview with Mary Coggenhoe produced nothing new. She merely repeated, as if they had discussed their evidence in advance, everything her husband had said. A parrot would have shown greater inventiveness. But talking to the pair of them crystallised one thought in Charlie's mind, and one of the notes he made back in his room later on read: "Their concern with their daughter is really a concern for themselves." Thinking it over he decided that wasn't so unusual.

The next person they called was Vibeke Nordli. She sat down confidently and expectantly, quite without the tension unconcealable in Rupert Coggenhoe. Attractive, ambitious, strong-minded. The details were unsurprising: born 1962, resident of Tromsø, married, one child, writing a thesis on Susannah Sneddon's novels, for which she expressed considerable enthusiasm.

"How did you hear about the Weekend?"

"I wrote to the Untamed Shrew Press, asking if they knew of any unpublished stuff — early novels, maybe one unfinished when she was murdered. They wrote back and said that *The Black Byre* was just completed when she was killed, and was published posthumously. They didn't know of any unpublished stuff. I had this feeling from the letter of — I don't know — of a sort of starchiness, stiffness. I would guess that they weren't going to be the publishers of the new edition. But anyway they mentioned Suzman, and said there was going to be this Weekend in Micklewike, so I wrote to High Maddox Farm."

"I suppose seeing the farm was a big attraction?"

"Yes, it was — and all the countryside around. For the thesis I was more interested in the manuscripts, of course, but seeing where she grew up, lived, the places that she wrote about — yes, that was an attraction."

"Is anyone writing the biography?" Charlie suddenly asked, from his inconspicuous chair at one side, where he was taking notes. "Or perhaps a joint biography of the pair of them?"

"Not that I know of."

Charlie looked at Oddie.

"A lot of people seem interested in the manuscripts. But I didn't hear one mention of a biography during the Weekend. You'd think if there was that much interest in her — in her and Joshua — someone would be writing her life."

"I don't know," said Vibeke Nordli, her forehead crinkling. "Comparing manuscripts with the printed texts is a comparatively straightforward matter, and not particularly time-consuming. Writing a life is a much bigger undertaking — particularly if it's a first one. You'd have to be really committed to take it on."

"You talked to Suzman, didn't you?" Oddie asked.

"Just briefly, when we did the tour of the farm. I'm afraid he didn't say anything of interest . . . It was odd: I somehow didn't get any sense of a strong personal interest in the Sneddons."

"You were puzzled as to why he was doing all this?"

"Frankly, yes. It didn't bother me for more than a moment or two at the time, but now that he's been murdered . . ."

Quite, thought the two policemen to themselves.

The next witness was Vidkun Mjølhus. His passport told them the personal details: born 1946, a bookseller, height, weight, and picture — the last showing he had not changed much in the eight years since it was taken. Though he was bulky, and had a bit more flesh on him than ideally he should, he was handsome, boyish and healthy. Yet Charlie thought as he sat there waiting for their questions that he was not entirely relaxed, not easy in the way that Vibeke Nordli had been.

"Oh yes, the Sneddon nowels go down werry big in Norvay. Susannah's, naturally. Two of them vos translated many years since. Nineteen thirty-five and six."

"So the new paperbacks sell well?"

"Werry vel."

"In English?"

"Yes, in English. Vee all read English — a little. But they start to be translated into Norwegian as well, the other ones. *Den Svarte Fjøs* has just been given out. *The Black Byre* — the last one. Werry popular."

"Why, do you think?"

"Norvay is a rural country. Even if vee live in towns, vee go back to our roots in our minds, vee have a bit of the peasant in us still, and vee long to go back vere vee come from — at Easter to ski, to fish in summer. Vee are not *easy* in towns, it does not feel *natural*."

"I see. And that's why you came to the Sneddon Weekend?"

"Accurate! . . . Sorry, I mean exactly. Excuse my English. I read the nowels, see they are in this vonderful tradition — like our Hamsun, Vesaas, and many others. And then I see a piece in *The Bookseller* — I get the publications for English bookshops, naturally, because I do business vith England — I see this piece about the Veekend and I say to myself: 'I take a little holiday.' "

"And did you talk to Mr Suzman during the Weekend?"

He grimaced and shook his head.

"No — is not my type. Werry smooth. Vibeke — she talk to him about the nowels. But I — no." He turned to Charlie. "I only see vot you see, hear vot you hear."

"Why," said Charlie when he had gone, "do I get the impression that he's holding something back?"

"Or not telling the whole truth? Or not telling the truth at all?" agreed Mike. "It's more difficult to tell plausible lies in a foreign tongue."

"Vibeke says he's a second-hand bookseller. It's difficult to imagine him having much to do with the new Sneddon boom."

"Of course he didn't actually say he did," said Oddie. "Not professionally. He presented it mainly as a personal thing . . . Though I can't see why he would do a lot of business with Britain, as he says he does." He looked down at the jotted notes he had made during the interview.

"Something strikes you that passed me by?" asked Charlie.

"Maybe . . . I wonder how many Norwegians born in 1946 were given the Christian name of Vidkun."

"Why on earth shouldn't they be?"

"It was the Christian name of Quisling."

Chapter 11

Questions (II)

Mrs Cardew, the Fellowship Secretary, was a useless witness. She kept insisting that Gerald Suzman's death could have nothing to do with the Fellowship, could not be a consequence of the "most successful" Weekend, and said over and over that the new organisation was the brainchild of devoted and tireless workers with not a thought of self. If anyone had suggested the dear old "passing tramp" she would have embraced the idea enthusiastically, so anxious was she to distance herself and the new literary society from the gruesome deed in Oxenthorpe. Both men got the impression that she might be in the lists against Rupert Coggenhoe in any moves to take over the Fellowship.

Mrs Marsden was another matter. A strong-minded countrywoman, she was clearly both more sensible and more intelligent than Mrs

172

Cardew, though certainly less well-educated. She made it plain she had been pleased to be offered the curator's post by Mr Suzman, had worked with him and for him devotedly and efficiently, but for all that she had never lost her clear-sightedness in relation to him and his doings.

"By the time I got involved he'd already bought the farm," she explained to Oddie and Charlie. "So I don't know much about that, apart from what I knew from living in the village."

"And that was?"

"That it was a pretty run-down affair. It had been farmed for years by the son of the man who bought it at the auction in 1933. He got sick a few years back, never let go of the reins, and eventually died. Mr Suzman bought it at a knockdown price, what with agriculture being in the state it is in at the moment, and the general recession. He's leased out most of the fields to other farmers, just keeping the bits around the farm and the spinney where Joshua shot himself. All in all, I don't suppose he laid out that much money."

"What about equipping it as a museum?"

"He enjoyed that, did Mr Suzman. It was like a bit of fun for him. He went to a lot of sales and auctions all round the country, buying up old stuff. But you wouldn't be talking high prices. He was just after the sort of furniture and kitchen utensils and stuff like that that they might have had."

"Was none of it actual stuff owned by the Sneddons?"

"Well . . ." There came on her the hesitation of honest doubt. "There were the two little tables that served as desks, for example. One was possibly Susannah's, the other definitely Joshua's, so he said."

"But you're not so sure?"

"It didn't look old enough to me. Like the American lady said, everything they had was old even then — fetched nothing at the auction after they died, so my mother always said. So I did just wonder — well, if he said it was definitely Joshua's because *some*thing had to be authentically his."

Mike Oddie nodded.

"But do you think, speaking as a countrywoman, that on the whole he did a good job with the place?"

"Yes, I do. That's the sort of way farmhouses looked back in the years between the wars. 'Course, I remember thinking, just before the Weekend, that what it didn't have was the dirt and the smells, or only faint echoes of them. There'd've been pigs and hens quite close to the farmhouse in those

174

days. But what can you do about farmyard smells, short of buying some kind of artificial spray? No, I'd say the place gave people some idea of what a farmhouse looked like back in the days when the Sneddons were alive."

"You remember them, don't you?"

"Yes, just. I don't set much store by that. Just having Susannah pointed out to me in the street by my mother as the woman who wrote books. What I really remember was all the talk after they died."

"What did people say?" Charlie asked.

"Well, of course they talked about it for years. A murder and a suicide in a little place like Micklewike — naturally it was a sensation. You're from the city, young man, I can hear that, and you wouldn't under-stand. What did people say? Well, they said he must have been jealous of her for years, her being so much more successful than him, and that finally he'd snapped. And I've never heard anything to show as we were wrong."

"I suppose you read the novels after Mr Suzman asked you to be curator?"

"Yes, I did. I'm not a great reader as a rule. I enjoyed them. I liked reading about the places that I recognised, and the sort of people that I know — or used to know, because times change, don't they, and people with them. Of course she exaggerated, like, but writers do that, don't they? No, I really enjoyed them, for all I was reading them as part of my job."

"And Mr Suzman himself: what did you think of him?"

She considered the question seriously. She was the sort of person who did not make judgments lightly.

"I didn't *know* him. He was my employer, he always treated me well, was always considerate. Beyond that . . ."

"He was a mystery?"

"Not exactly that, but he was from another sort of life, wasn't he? One that I know nothing about. He always wanted me to call him Gerald, but somehow I never could. 'Sir' came much more natural. People I called by their Christian names would be — well, different sorts of people."

"Why do you think he was so active in setting up the Sneddon Fellowship?"

"I can't say I know, for all we talked about it so much. I suppose he thought highly of the books."

"You don't think there was something in it for him?"

"Well . . . not to speak ill of the dead . . . but you've got your job to do, and *some*one killed him, and someone must have had a reason . . . Well, I wouldn't have said he was the kind to do something for nothing. Yes, I would guess that there was something in it for him, but what it was I never got any hint. Could it have been some kind of honour? Like from the Queen?"

But neither Mike nor Charlie thought he was in it for an OBE.

Mike Oddie liked Gillian Parkin at once. Frank, open, enthusiastic — he could see that she and Vibeke Nordli would get on, quite apart from their shared interests: they were similar types.

"As soon as I heard about the setting-up of the Fellowship I knew I had to come along," she said, settling into her chair. "I've been working on the thesis for a year now, and I'm sort of saturated in Susannah Sneddon."

"What about the chap who was with you in the pub on Friday?" asked Charlie.

"My bloke? His name is Gregory Waite. No interest in the Sneddons at all. Botanist, London University, like me. He was happy to come along, then to take off on a walking tour round Yorkshire. He'll be back on Thursday or Friday — I'm booked into the Black Horse until then."

"Why did you decide to stay so long?"

"It's the best chance I've had to see the places that she wrote about. I'm ashamed to say I've never been to Yorkshire before. It's good to meet up with people like Vibeke who really know the novels. If you do research on Dickens there are people all around you with the same interest. With Susannah Sneddon you're on your own. This Weekend was a chance to feel less lonely."

"Your particular interest is in the manuscripts, isn't it?" Charlie asked. Gillian Parkin grinned, as if this was some kind of dark secret, and she had been found out.

"OK, that's another reason for staying on a bit. I knew there were typescripts, knew they were being edited for a new edition, so I thought I might winkle my way in and get a share of the action. Anything wrong in that?"

"Nothing at all."

"When I saw the pages he had put out in the Museum I was even more keen. It wasn't just a matter of correcting errors; there was obviously lots of new stuff — things that had been cut out. Censorship. She was cut by her publishers because she was saying things that women weren't *allowed* to say at that time. Yes — I was very keen to get my hands on those typescripts."

"So you approached Mr Suzman?" Mike Oddie asked.

"Yes, I did. Twice — no, three times."

"What was his reaction?"

"Cool. Distant. The general drift of what he said was that everything was in hand, the typescripts were being edited — by him, I gathered, and lucky little me would have the benefit of reading them when, one by one, they are published."

"No special favours?"

"That was the gist. A courteous brush-off. That's why I got Vibeke to propose me for the steering committee of the Fellowship. I thought it would give me a bit of leverage. Obviously he wasn't going to ask me to edit one of the books, or establish a definitive text, but maybe he'd give me an advance look at the proofs or whatever."

"When Vibeke Nordli heard he was dead her first reaction was: what's going to happen to the new edition of the novels?" said Charlie. "Would you say that was your reaction too?"

"Yes."

"You didn't care for Suzman?"

"I thought he was a creep."

"Creep covers a lot of ground. What sort of creep?"

"You sound like my supervisor: 'To convey

a meaning language must be used precisely.' All right, fair enough: what sort of a creep? The sort who looks up women's skirts, given half a chance. He had a letch for Vibeke, by the way. The sort who smarms, who would call you 'dear lady' except that he knows any feminist would brain him if he did, the sort who is in it for himself — a sort of literary limpet. It so happens that he picked on Susannah Sneddon to suck blood out of, but it could just as easily have been Jeffrey Archer or Barbara Taylor Bradford. Literary values just didn't enter into it."

"But what was the blood he was getting out of Susannah Sneddon?"

She shook her head and shrugged.

"Search me. But there was blood, I'll bet."

"Or would have been, if he hadn't been killed," said Charlie.

"Right . . . Right," said Gillian Parkin, for the first time uncertain. "I suppose there's got to be a motive there somewhere, but I don't get what it could be."

Lettie Farraday came last, and made no bones about her enjoyment of the murder enquiry. Mike Oddie saw at once what had attracted Charlie to her, and understood his feelings of protectiveness.

"You've no idea what *fun* it is down there

in the bar!" she said, levering herself down heavily into the chair with Charlie's help. "The fuss, the people! The landlord's all but purring, and he's put on three extra bar staff. There's an old boy there — Len Trubshaw is his name — that I went to school with down here in Batley Bridge. He was the sort of little boy who loved pulling the girls' hair and making them cry. He's sitting there just lapping up all the scandal and innuendo and conjecture."

"So are you, Lettie," said Charlie mischievously.

"In a different way. Just show a bit more respect for age, Dexter."

"When did you go to school with him, Mrs Farraday?" Oddie asked.

"The late 'twenties. When George V was on the throne. Are you asking exactly how old I am?"

"Yes."

"Dexter knows. I was born in 1917. So I was a little kid of five and upwards when Susannah and Joshua were writing all those novels."

"So you have a lot more memories of them than Mrs Marsden, say?"

"Is that the curator? Oh yes, sure. I can't say I remember her, but I'd guess she was a good ten years younger than me. A girl of fifteen, about to stretch her wings and fly the nest, doesn't take much notice of a five-year-old."

"Is that the age you were when you left?"

"Yes, sir! Soon as I decently could. I went as a maid to a woman in Halifax, because it was live-in, and I knew she was about to move to London. Five years later it was the USA."

"How did that come about?" Charlie asked.

"Don't ask! But knowing you I suppose you'll guess that good old s.e.x. was involved."

"What made you decide to come back?"

"Oh, I come back regularly. I come back to Europe every year, though I can't say that Britain is my favourite place to come to. I decided to include Micklewike this year because I read an article about the Weekend and the Sneddon cult in *Time* magazine. I decided I wanted to be part of it."

"Why? Were you suspicious?" Charlie asked.

"No. Why should I be?"

"The police have been suspicious of Suzman for a long time."

"I'm not police. I don't think I'd be a lot of use to the law-enforcement agencies. No, it was just *interest*. Tinged with vanity,

I suppose. I realized I was one of the people who did know a bit about the Sneddons. They weren't well-known in the village because they weren't liked. People would never have dropped in and called on them. Just because my mother went up there to clean the place meant I knew more about them than most."

"And yet from what I hear from Charlie, Suzman wasn't particularly interested in your memories," said Oddie.

"No, he wasn't. Maybe I was just flattering myself thinking that he would be. Perhaps he was just interested in the books, not the Sneddons' lives. Remember the woman in the Thurber cartoon: 'Mere proof won't convince me!' Maybe he wasn't interested in mere facts about them. But in that case why buy High Maddox Farm, and why set up the Museum at all?"

"I've been wondering why nobody seems to be writing a biography," put in Charlie.

"Right. With all that sensational material to end up with it does seem odd. Maybe I shall write down what I remember, and leave it with this curator person."

"What was your opinion of the Museum?" Oddie asked.

"I've talked about this with Dexter, and at the meeting. Too clean, too hygienic, too antiseptic. Suzman and whoever helped him with it *tried* to give a feeling of a pretty disorderly household, but they didn't go nearly far enough. Susannah was a sloven, and the place was a tip. Perhaps it was inevitable they wouldn't get it right: those farmyard smells are gone today, and people would have been just nauseated walking round the farmhouse as it usually was before my mother got going on it. But there's another thing . . ."

"Yes?"

"It was rather like a stage set. Or a film set for *The Last Days of Susannah Sneddon*. When it came down to it there was very little of the Sneddons there. And what there was was sometimes wrong. As I said at the meeting, Susannah Sneddon didn't type. I'd confirmed this with my mother the night before. I expect someone in the village or down here in Batley Bridge typed up the manuscripts. But Mr Suzman obviously didn't know that."

"And he didn't follow it up when you told him," said Charlie.

"I expect he thought this was just the ramblings of an old lady with a lousy memory," said Lettie shrugging.

"Others didn't," Charlie pointed out. "As soon as I began introducing you as someone

184

who knew the Sneddons there was enormous interest."

"Right. Rather pleasing to the vanity I mentioned. Mind you, I don't think I made those fans very happy. I couldn't hide the fact that I just never liked Susannah Sneddon. That wasn't because my mother went on about her writing dirty books. If my mother said something I disagreed with her on principle, even if it had to be quietly. Looking back I find that Susannah was very self-absorbed, living a life cut off from the rest of us, so — as a child — I found her creepy. Now I'm older — much older! — I can admire her for achieving so much against the odds, but then I found her antipathetic."

"And Joshua?"

"Hardly ever saw him. But in the village he was not really liked. He wasn't understood, or sympathised with. They said the war had made him a bit strange. Though to be sure they always said he was harmless enough. Just prickly and odd."

"None of which, apparently, interested Gerald Suzman enough for him to want to talk to you," said Oddie thoughtfully. "I agree with Charlie: there's something here that doesn't add up."

"What about last night?" asked Charlie suddenly. "I asked you to put the chain on

185

the door and a chair in front of it. Did anything happen?"

Lettie's brow furrowed.

"I honestly don't think so. I didn't take you too seriously, and I slept. Yes — I did wake up now and again, and I could have been woken by something. But old people generally don't sleep that well. I know I don't. So waking up in the night is perfectly natural. I just thought — still think — you were scaremongering."

"Maybe I was," agreed Charlie. "I just sensed something."

"Oh, I'm not knocking 'just sensing something.' I do it myself. And you were right, weren't you? You just got the wrong victim."

When he was back in his room in Haworth Road and hunched over his little typewriter, Charlie wrote: "The wrong victim?" But then he shook his head. Gerald Suzman was a crook, and therefore murderable, even if they had not yet discovered a really concrete motive.

He wrote: "I do not know these people. I go by appearances." He thought: Gillian Parkin seems bright, open, quick-witted, uncomplicated. So does Vibeke Nordli. But are they? How do I know they are not greedy, power-mad, vengeful? I don't. I am accepting the surface they present to the world as a reality. In everyone there's an element of performance. I don't even *know* that Lettie is lame . . .

It was a depressing thought to go to bed on.

Chapter 12

The Unattractive Couple

The house they were looking for was called Sandringham, and it was somewhere along Ladysmith Street, in Ilkley, a street which wound maddeningly, edged by Edwardian villas well-shaded by shrubs from the prying vulgar. Solid, middle-class houses for solid, middle-class people, they boasted names rather than numbers. The whole street was a postman's nightmare, and Mike Oddie and Charlie Peace were getting decidedly fed-up with it too.

Charlie had had a late night, going over and over in his mind the interviews of the day before and typing up the meagre scraps of information and impressions that he thought might prove of interest. He had woken up bright as a button, though: he was well-used by now to the irregularities of police routine. His landlady had had the

188

pleasure of watching him eat a good half of his breakfast, and had done her best to pump him the while. Charlie, at his most genial and tantalising, had given her the sort of information that would be common knowledge in Batley Bridge by the end of the day, and in return Mrs Ludlum had promised that, even if he didn't need it that night, his room would be kept for him: "Just whenever you need it, Mr Peace, it'll be there." Charlie liked the feeling of being a prestige guest.

Later in the day they were off to London, to Mr Suzman's home base, but Mike Oddie had decided to let Scotland Yard — who had started the whole thing, after all — find some of the routine answers before they got there. It was just possible, he thought, that the Potter-Hodges had the answer to the curious incuriousness of Mr Suzman concerning the lives of Susannah and Joshua. Was he not so much indifferent to the details of their lives as determined to suppress or filter them?

It was now ten o'clock, as early as seemed decent for a police visit to a couple whose connections to Mr Suzman seemed at most tangential.

"There it is," said Charlie.

The name, considerately, had been put on

the gate, as the house itself was shrouded by dark green shrubs and trees — ivies, laurels, the darker kind of firs.

"They do go in for mountain greenery, don't they?" said Charlie, cheerfully.

He found another notice on the gate when he approached it: "Beware of the Dog." He experimentally clicked the latch and was rewarded by a thunderous peal of barking and a sound like the charge of a tank regiment. From round the side of the house, recklessly oblivious of branch and fern, careered an enormous Rottweiler, throwing itself against the gate from which Charlie had prudently retreated.

"Well, you're a fine fellow, aren't you? Or do I mean lady? What's your name, then? You're doing a good job here."

The dog thought, then tentatively waggled its rear and its end stump. Charlie, equally tentatively, advanced on the gate again, and the dog went off in an ecstasy of barking.

"Who is it, Zoë? Good girl — quiet now." Coming out from the front door was Felix Potter-Hodge. He advanced down the path to the gate, but stopped in bewilderment when he saw Charlie.

"Oh — weren't you at the Sneddon Weekend?"

"That's right," said Charlie, taking out

his ID. "West Yorkshire Police."

The man took it and inspected it, an expression of curiosity and puzzlement on his cratered face.

"*Really?* But . . . We'd heard he'd been killed, of course, but . . . Why were you at the Weekend? Does this mean? — "

"Do you think we could come in, Mr Potter-Hodge?" Oddie said, coming up from the car in which he had prudently stayed. "We've a few questions — it won't take long."

"Of course, of course. Down, Zoë — she's just a big softie, really. Yes, they're *friends*, Zoë. Come along in."

Gingerly they went through the gate, brushing aside the cold green branches and leaves, then down the front path towards the house — a confection of grey stone, awkward arched bays and lead-lighted windows and door. Once inside Mr Potter-Hodge called "Mavis" towards the kitchen and led them — Zoë blundering along very much in their way — through to a sitting-room furnished with a mixture of heavy old tables and cupboards and an anonymous modern sofa and chairs, with a television set as the central feature. It was a comfortable enough room, but without any sign of individual taste.

"Well!" said Mavis, as she came in after a whispered consultation with her husband in the hall. "We didn't expect . . ." She turned to Charlie and became almost roguish. "You *are* a dark horse, aren't you? Going to the Weekend as if you were a Sneddon fan, and being a policeman all the time. You put on a very good show, I'll give you that. But what were you there for, eh?"

"I think I'd better ask the questions," said Oddie hurriedly. "It'll all be clear in time. Perhaps I could start by asking you both the same question: what were you at the Weekend for?"

The pair sat down on the sofa, looked at each other, then at the policemen. Felix Potter-Hodge's face resembled some vandalised Gothic church: all cracks and craggy edges, with stubbly cheeks and chin and brown stubs for teeth. His long body seemed ill-coordinated, his hands claw-like. Mavis on the other hand sat there like a white meringue, a series of blobs waiting passively for someone who liked that sort of thing.

"Well," said Felix, "first of all, we're not great readers."

"That's right," said Mavis. "I'm afraid the telly's good enough for us."

"Except on Saturday night, of course."

192

"You go out on Saturday night?" Oddie asked.

"Oh no. I mean that nobody could find Saturday night telly good enough for them. Anyway, I've known as long as I can remember that my Gran was great friends with this woman who wrote novels. It was something Gran took pride in — though she never liked to talk about her death: it upset her too much. But she'd mention her, just dropping it into the conversation, like saying 'My friend Susannah Sneddon, the novelist,' though more often than not the name meant nothing at all to the person she was speaking to. But the name started coming up, now and again, in the years after she died, either because of the novels, or because of the murder case."

"There's talk of a television series from one of the novels," said Mavis, in the tone of one who thought that this was the fictional equivalent of beatification.

"That's right," said her husband, nodding complacently, "there is. That'll be good for Micklewike. Anyway, when I inherited this house from my father, along with the grocery business — Ilkley's the sort of place where you can still keep a good *family* grocery business going, and we do very nicely — well, we went through everything, because my Dad had been a bit of a hoarder and collector, and he loved anything to do with the family."

"It was Felix's father who was responsible for the 'Potter-Hodge' thing," said Mavis apologetically. "Felix's Gran was Mrs Potter, but she'd been a Miss Hodge. His father said the family had always been men of substance in Ilkley, so he added his mother's name to make it sound grander. But it doesn't, does it? It's a bit of an embarrassment, really."

"So when we were going through all this junk — cuttings about my Granddad when he was Mayor of Ilkley, that sort of thing — it was a bit touch-and-go whether we'd throw out this pile of letters from Susannah Sneddon. She was nothing to us, to be perfectly frank. But as luck would have it we sat down and read through one or two of them, and — I don't know — "

"We just thought," said Mavis, "that they were something out of the ordinary. I mean, we're not scholars or anything, but we could tell these weren't just the usual letters between friends, the sort of people who used to write regularly, but don't any more because they phone instead. They were — well — so nicely written, so vivid, they gave you such a good picture of what her life was like, how she wrote the books. There was nothing run-of-the-mill about them."

"So, to cut a long story short, we decided to keep them. We've got this big house with just us rattling round in it. There's no shortage of storage space. Then we started hearing her name mentioned, didn't we, Mavis?"

"That's right, like I said. In the papers, even on TV and a little piece on her and Micklewike in *The Yorkshire Countryside*. People were starting to get interested. So when we heard about the Sneddon Weekend we thought we'd go along."

"We got down the letters and had another peek, and it struck us we really had something to contribute."

Watching these two ill-favoured people chattering on, so happy with their tiny corner of literary history, it suddenly struck Charlie that his view of them had been horribly coloured by the fact of their physical unattractiveness: it was not nice to look into the gaping hole of Felix Potter-Hodge's mouth and see his discoloured teeth; Mavis's plump and placid whiteness was that bit off-putting. And yet they seemed perfectly ordinary people, with simple pleasures and no discernible malice.

It was the converse of his thought of the night before: if Gillian Parkin and Vibeke

Nordli had blinded him — as perhaps they had — by being healthy, handsome and open people on the surface, had not this pair done the same by being so physically off-putting? They might be dull, conventional, constitutionally lethargic types and still be morally above reproach. A policeman should not come with an in-built bias in favour of beautiful people. Reality, in his experience, was all the time conflicting with appearance. He had personally arrested many handsome people of both sexes.

"And I gather when you mentioned the letters, Gerald Suzman was interested?" Oddie was asking. The two nodded vigorously.

"Oh yes, very much so," said Mavis complacently. "Wanted to acquire them for his Museum."

"But you wouldn't sell?"

"Well, we didn't want to rush into selling, at any rate," said Felix cautiously. "I mean, it was the opposite way round to the usual: the more interest he showed, the less we wanted to sell — not because we wanted to make them more valuable and stick out for a high price, but because, well, we liked having some part in this literary figure people were talking about, and we didn't feel like giving it up at once."

"We said we'd lend," said Mavis, nodding

like a doll to everything her husband said. "We'd have been quite happy to have a letter — or more, even — on exhibition at the farm, on more or less permanent loan."

"There are quite a number of them, you see. And we made it quite clear that we'd be willing to make them available to anyone doing work on Susannah Sneddon — like scholars and reporters, and anyone writing a book."

"But we wanted to keep them, at least for the moment. They're a bit of history that is ours."

Zoë came in heavily from the hall, and muzzled her big head in Mavis's lap, her round eyes straying shamelessly to a box of chocolates on the side table.

"She's just a big softie, you see," said Mavis fondly, opening the box and selecting one. "Who's a lucky girl, then?"

"Just how keen was Suzman to buy the letters?" asked Oddie. "Did you talk about it just the once?"

"Oh no. He phoned us on the Saturday evening, late on: very interested he was, and hoping to see the letters. We said there wasn't any problem about that. Then on the Sunday, after the meeting, we were going back to our car, intending to drive back here, because we didn't fancy the lecture, and he drove past, stopped, and insisted that we went to lunch with him."

"It was Chinese," said Mavis. "Not what we'd have chosen."

"It was very nice of him," insisted Felix. "But I always say you don't know what you're eating."

"You say it was nice of him, but he was still after the letters?"

"Oh yes, but he didn't have to buy us lunch, did he? Oh, he was after them all right, and getting down to figures by the time we had coffee."

"What kind of figures?"

"Well, it started at three thousand, and it was up to five by the time he was driving us back to Micklewike."

"Sight unseen?"

"Yes. He'd never seen any of them."

"But you didn't accept?"

"No. The most we would say was that we might think about it in two or three years' time."

"Did that satisfy him?"

"Well, it had to, didn't it? He couldn't make us sell. But we could tell he wasn't happy."

"I'm finding his interest that bit odd," said Mike, "because apparently he was otherwise not at all interested in the biographical details of the Sneddons, or facts about their daily life."

"He might have been planning to publish the letters," Charlie pointed out. "If he owned them he could do that, couldn't he? And there might be a bit of money in it. Did he mention the possibility?"

"Oh no," said Mavis. "Just the fact that they ought to be at the farm."

"Really he played his cards very close to his chest," said Felix.

Zoë suddenly leapt up and charged out the living-room door into the hall, barking like a machine-gun. The two policemen nearly jumped out of their chairs.

"Just the milkman," said Mavis. "He's shockingly late by the time he gets to us."

"You can't tell her not to," said Felix, "because that's what we keep her for, isn't it?"

"Half the time it's just a cat, though," said Mavis. "Like Sunday night."

The policemen pricked up their ears.

"Sunday night?"

"Put on a great performance just after we'd got into bed. Felix got up, but there wasn't anybody."

"You're sure?" asked Oddie, turning to her husband.

"Just someone walking down the road some

way away. Looked perfectly respectable. It was probably next-door's cat set her off."

"I think," said Oddie, "that, just to be on the safe side, we'd better take those letters into safe keeping."

The two looked outraged, as if he'd proposed to take their baby into custody.

"Oh surely," protested Felix, "I mean, that can't be necessary, can it? Nobody can know what's in them, so they can't be after them."

"Perhaps it's someone who *fears* what's in them," Oddie pointed out. "Look, this is what I'd suggest: what if we take them to Ilkley police station, and ask them to keep them there for a while, and take photocopies: one for you and one for us. Then you could deposit either the originals or the copy with your bank. If you lose the originals entirely you lose your part in the whole Sneddon business — the books, the new fame, the murder."

They thought about that, and then nodded. Felix went to the sideboard, bent down and brought out an old, collapsing cardboard box that had "Seagrim's Luncheon Meat" printed on the side. The letters lay in four substantial piles, without envelopes, each one a thick wodge of paper. On top of them were three very amateur snapshots, all three of a heavy-looking woman, posing awkwardly against

200

different backgrounds: High Maddox Farm; the little wood nearby; and a long, low hedge-row. Oddie took up one of the letters at random and Charlie, looking over his shoulder, read it with him:

> *High Maddox Farm,*
> *March 19th 1932.*

Dear Janet,
Well, the book is done, finished in rough draft at any rate. Much work still to be done on it. As usual at this stage I don't know whether it is good or bad, saleable or a drug on the market. Joshua, at least, *always knows!* He has one ready to send to the publishers — beautifully typed and to me quite incomprehensible. He is melancholy about it, but quite resigned, Also, he can't think of a title. Titles are so important. I am calling mine *The Black Byre.* It has a ring about it, doesn't it?

And so Spring is coming. I feel it in the air, even here, in our high, wind-swept village. It is not the meagre crocuses in the cottage patches in Mickle-wike that tell me that the earth is re-newing itself once more, but the tang and zest of the breezes that blow across the valley. Joshua feels it as he ploughs his furrows, thinking his Modernist thoughts, and I feel it as I walk through the spinney and out to the moorlands, wondering whether the earth will give me one more tale to spin . . .

The two men looked at each other.
"I don't think she sounds like a very nice woman," said Charlie.

Chapter 13

Cousin of Some Sort

The trip to London went very well. They said at Leeds/Bradford airport that they only had one spare seat on the twelve o'clock flight, but there quite often were cancellations. When they got to the makeshift little structure they found a Leeds businessman being decanted into an ambulance after a minor heart attack. "Dirty old sod!" Charlie heard one immaculately coiffed air hostess mutter to another. "Shan't have to worry about his hands for a month or two!" At Heathrow they found the car they had requested from Scotland Yard waiting for them: Charlie's friend Superintendent Trethowan was both interested and grateful, and he made that clear in the talk and exchange of information they had in his office an hour later, en route for for Gerald Suzman's flat in Dolphin Square.

The flat had a view over the Thames towards Battersea and the sad defacement of the power station. Sitting snugly between the Tate Gallery and Chelsea the flat itself belied its bland exterior by being undoubtedly the home of an artist of sorts, though certainly a self-indulgent rather than a rigorously disciplined one: there were plush, soft carpets, silk shirts and dressing-gowns, gastronomic delicacies from Harrods. There were books everywhere, especially expensive art books, which looked like complimentary copies of volumes which Suzman had been concerned with in some way, some having grateful personal inscriptions. Everything in the flat spoke of — nay, announced in a loud voice — the amateur litterateur, the epicurean, the connoisseur.

Nothing, however, spoke of criminal activities.

"I suppose you wouldn't expect to find traces *here*," said Oddie dispiritedly. "If he puts together, say, an early, privately printed edition of a Matthew Arnold poem — "

"No 'say' about it: he did," said Charlie.

"Right. But not so as to be convicted in a court of law. Anyway, you wouldn't expect to find copies here. Similarly if he'd produced a choice piece of Swinburne erotica apparently printed for circulation to the poet's similarly inclined friends, you wouldn't expect him to treasure a copy for himself — especially as his tastes certainly don't seem to have taken him in that particular direction. No, he'd want to sell the small number he produced, and not keep any incriminating evidence."

"It's disappointing, though, that there's so little correspondence, and no financial records."

"Any dubious transactions would be done on the 'phone, I imagine. The telephone is the great avoider of written records. The bank may give us some idea of how much his activities raked in, but not what the activities were, or who the money came from."

"The big things are well in the past," Charlie pointed out. "The Brontë booklets and the sexy Byron letters. Those were way back in the 'sixties."

"That doesn't mean there haven't been big things that nobody has cast doubts on," said Oddie. "He may simply have got better at it. We might get more idea about that from his bank. I doubt whether we'll find out much from either of his bookshops. Someone who is obviously keen to cover his traces wouldn't leave anything of interest in such obvious places."

"One's just off Piccadilly, isn't it? Where is the other?"

"Pocklington — little village in Sussex. I'm sure both will be meeting places, places to conclude deals at, but I doubt whether there'll be anything in the records. Of course the managers just *might* talk, now that he's dead."

"And the heir is a godson aged five," said Charlie, going over in his mind the information that Trethowan had produced for them at Scotland Yard, "That doesn't sound very promising."

"No. Though the question 'Who benefits?' obviously has to include his parents in the answer, rather than the boy himself. Jonathan Charlton his name is. What did Trethowan say? His father is something in publishing, isn't he?"

"Yes — I suppose that could be interesting, some sort of connection. What next, boss?"

Mike Oddie screwed up his face.

"While we're down in London we have to see the boy's parents, and we'll need to talk to Randolph Sneddon. We'll go along and see the bookshop manager in Mandeville Street, and if possible the one in Sussex too. Meantime we'll hope that Scotland Yard will come up with something meaty on his financial position. I'll get on the phone now and try to set some things up."

The dossier of information provided by the Yard told Oddie that the stockbroking firm in the City which employed Randolph Sneddon was called Massingham Richards, and that it had a better-than-average reputation. The impression of respectability was confirmed by Sneddon himself: his response to Oddie's call was friendly, but he said that police on the premises of a stockbroking firm was something (especially these days, with all the trouble at Lloyds) to be avoided at all costs. He made an appointment with the policemen at his Notting Hill flat for six o'clock that evening. Mrs Charlton, the mother of the heir to whatever Suzman had left, sounded young and bright, though she also claimed to be "very upset" by Suzman's death. She said she was "flat out" for the rest of the day, but agreed to see them next morning at ten. She added that she had no idea of the sort of sum that would be involved in the Suzman legacy, but said that Suzman had always given her the impression of someone who lived up to his income.

The bookshop was a disappointment: it was very smart, very well-stocked with collectable books, and its manager was very bland. A modern office block was, by comparison, communicative. The man admitted under forceful questioning that he had heard "a rumour or two" about Mr Suzman's activities in the literary world, but the dead man had kept anything of that sort quite distinct from his activities in the shop; otherwise, the manager said, he would have severed any connection with him. "I'm just a simple bookseller," he said, with a smile that verged on the nervous, "and I manage the place for him." And as far as they could tell from the investigation of shop records and invoices that was the truth — the superficial truth, if not the underlying one.

It was clear as soon as they drew up outside Randolph Sneddon's flat that it was a very desirable one. They were in the best part of Notting Hill, and the house was an impeccably renovated nineteenth century one: three stories and an attic, spick and span as if it had been built yesterday. Beside the door there were only four bells. They were a few minutes early, and they got no response when they tried the bell marked "Sneddon." As they stood waiting, though, an elderly lady, dressed for an evening out, came out of the door and smiled at them.

"Was it Mr Sneddon you wanted? I heard the bell as I came down the stairs. I imagine he'll be home soon. Rush hour traffic is hell these days."

"Our appointment's not till six," said Oddie.

"Yorkshire . . ." said the woman pensively. "The Sneddon Conference. You wouldn't be policemen, would you?"

"Well — "

"Of course you are. Funny how you can always tell, isn't it? Policemen have a certain . . . aura, I suppose. Well, I think it's rather a splendid murder. It has all the ingredients, which so few do these days. Odd to be nostalgic for the murders of one's girlhood, isn't it? I'll be very sad if Mr Sneddon did it, but he'll make a perfectly lovely suspect. *What* a handsome man!"

"Heathcliff, one lady suggested," put in Charlie.

"Yes . . . Or Mr Rochester. Or, better still, Lord Byron. There's something very raffish there — gambling, hordes of women, fast cars. Something deliciously beyond the pale of respectable society. Oh — here he is."

She gave him a sweet-old-lady smile as she passed him, but he was dashing along after locking his Porsche and did not notice. He was profuse in his apologies.

"Can't tell you how sorry I am. There were hold-ups all the way. Can't imagine why everyone has to take their cars to work

209

these days. Come along up . . . Here we are."

His flat occupied the whole of the first floor. After a spacious entry hall they were led into a very large living room, furnished mainly in black leather, with a plethora of dark wooden side tables scattered all around, all seeming to be waiting for drinks to be set down on them. The pictures on the wall were modern, but displayed no particular taste — reproductions of a Hockney, a Lucien Freud, a rather pallid abstract. Through open doorways Charlie caught a glimpse of a fair-sized dining room and two bedrooms with capacious beds. In contrast to Mr Suzman's flat, there was not a sign of a book anywhere to be seen. This is a very high-class bachelor pad, thought Charlie to himself, and the bachelor prefers to live rather than read.

"Well!" said Randolph Sneddon, throwing himself on to the sofa, having fixed himself a whiskey and water after his offer of a drink for them had been refused. "What do you want to know? Silly question: of course you want to know about Mr Suzman, and I've been racking my brains as to what I do know about him. Because he was rather a cagey bird — or he was in my few dealings with him. Well, he lived in Dolphin Square — I don't suppose that's news to you — "

"What about if I ask the questions, sir," Mike Oddie said. "Then we can find out if there's anything I've missed at the end. How long have you known Mr Suzman?"

"I'm not sure I can be said to have *known* him at all. How long have he and I been in contact? That should be easy enough." He got up with athletic grace and went over to the telephone table by the door to consult an engagement diary. "We first met for a proper conversation five months ago at the Groucho Club."

"His place or yours?"

"Very definitely his. We'd been in telephone and written contact for a week or two before that."

"How did that come about?"

"Well, initially it was by letter — I expect I've got it somewhere if you want to see it. He wrote asking if I was the Randolph Sneddon whose grandfather had been cousin to Susannah Sneddon the novelist."

"How had he found that out?"

"Some kind of genealogical research, I think. My grandfather had moved down to Essex in the 'thirties, and set up a small building firm, which my father took over after his death. My father was fairly prominent in the Romford Conservative Association. It wouldn't have been difficult."

"Anything else in the letter?"

"Oh, some stuff about a new interest in her work, and so on. I wrote back and said that I was her whatever-it-is cousin, but that I really had no info about her. I was born in 1960, my grandfather was dead, my father told me no more than the basic facts about Susannah and Joshua. After that Suzman phoned me, told me about his plans for the Weekend, and invited me to lunch."

"Why did you accept?"

Sneddon shrugged his broad shoulders and frowned.

"Why indeed? It's a fascinating story, of course. I think my father was always more proud of being associated with a sensational murder-suicide than with a not-very-well-known writer. And then again it's family. Most of the chaps where I work have family of a rather different sort. I suppose I thought it was a step in the right direction — interesting, scandalous, if hardly distinguished."

"So you met him for lunch: how did he strike you?"

He frowned again, as if unused to describing people, except in the most conventional terms, or simply by the extent of their money.

"Well . . . not the sort I'm used to, frankly, so I'm rather at a loss . . . I mean, here we were in the Groucho, with people all around that I'd heard of, or knew from the box. That *Private Eye* man was there, getting pie-eyed on treacle tart. And that young actor from *Heavy Metal*. It was all . . . arty, I suppose you'd say. Not the world I know at all, but somehow flattering to be in. Something to talk about with friends afterwards."

"But what about Suzman himself?"

"Well, the same goes for him; he was arty, very sophisticated, very much at home in that world, greeting friends, pointing out celebrities or people I felt I should have heard of. So it was, as I say, rather exciting, the sort of thing I knew I'd boast about next day, or let drop ever so casually."

"You're something in the City, aren't you?"

"That's right. I sit in front of a screen watching figures change upwards or downwards. What used to be called a Yuppie until our world collapsed."

"So you were seduced by a different sort of world to your own?"

He smiled a smile of devastating, saturnine charm.

"Not exactly seduced, Superintendent. But I did agree to do what he wanted."

"Which was?"

"Oh, nothing very strenuous. He wanted me to tag along to this Weekend thing and represent the family. Well, there was no one else who could do it. My father died a couple of years ago, by the way. And Suzman made me feel in an odd way rather, well, chuffed. Silly damned feeling, but there it is: she was my whatever-it-is cousin, and all those people would be coming because they love her books. Childish for *me* to feel chuffed, but I did, so I said yes. And I did my bit: I read a couple of the books."

"Boned up on family history?"

"Well, that was a bit more difficult: nobody to ask."

"Wasn't it talked about at all when you were a child?"

"Hardly at all. As I said, I never knew my grandfather. My father did no more than mention that there was a novelist in the family, because he didn't remember her and had no special information on the murder-suicide. So any info I had on the family I got from Gerald Suzman, not vice versa."

"And that was the extent of your knowledge of Suzman before the Weekend?"

"The odd extra letter later on, with details — otherwise yes."

"You trusted him?"

He raised his eyebrows in a gesture which

in other circumstances must have been devastating.

"Why not? What was it to me? If you mean, do I think he was in general a man to trust, I'd say: as much as most. In the City we never trust anybody all the way down the line."

"We feel the same way in the CID," murmured Oddie. "So, when you went up to Yorkshire, what happened there?"

"Well, most of it you'll have been told," said Sneddon, gesturing towards Charlie.

"You weren't surprised to see Detective Constable Peace, I noticed, when we turned up on your doorstep," slipped in Oddie.

"No, I wasn't. I was rung up last night by Mrs Cardew, the Fellowship Secretary. I must say I was intrigued. Not something I expected at all. I won't ask why he was at the Weekend, because I know I won't be told . . . Well, I put up at the Duke of Cumberland, as you know. Suzman came down on the Friday evening and we had a good talk. He emphasized I was there to represent the family, and suggested I had a bit of family lore at my fingertips: 'There's a family tradition that Susannah was a terrible cook' — that sort of thing. If there was such a tradition it never got to me, but that's by the way."

"It didn't worry you, this kind of deception?"

He spread out his soft hands.

"Harmless enough, I thought. A bit like talking up shares on the Stock Exchange."

"And the rest of the weekend?"

"Well — you'll have seen." He had turned again to Charlie. "Talking to devotees, getting better at it as the days wore on, making up my own family traditions — nothing elaborate or damaging, just adding to the harmless stock of Sneddon lore. In the end I got landed on the Committee, but I didn't mind. It was beginning to seem like a great laugh."

"Did you have much to do with Gerald Suzman?"

"Not much during the actual events. He was always here and there talking to participants, as I was. I was hoping to get hold of him at the end, but I got buttonholed and somehow missed him. So I went along to see him at his cottage — you'll have been told about that?"

Oddie nodded non-committally. "You knew where he lived?"

"He gave me a map on the Friday — a simple one connecting Micklewike with the cottage at Oxenthorpe. I like a good, fast country drive. It was no problem finding the place. We had a talk about the Com-

216

mittee meetings, and I had to emphasize that my job in the City came first — I'd get to the meetings if I could, but I have my living to earn, and a damned difficult one it is too, in this recession. I told him I'd get there if I could, but I hadn't a great deal to contribute, and he might have to regard me as something of a figurehead. That seemed fine by him — he said it was the name he wanted. Then a neighbour came about something and I said goodbye."

"How did you spend the rest of the evening?"

"Had a drink in the bar at the Cumberland — someone will have remembered seeing me. That was eight-thirty, nineish. Showered, went to bed for a few hours' sleep, then up at four to drive to London, so as to be at work yesterday morning."

"Is there anything more you can tell us about Gerald Suzman?"

He considered. "Not facts, no. Impressions? He was probably a phoney, but a very entertaining one. He used to say mildly amusing things: 'Be a Sneddon, dear boy — it's your mission in life.' That kind of thing. All things considered, I shall miss him. And I suppose I'll even miss the Fellowship, if it's wound up."

"You knew he owned the farm?"

"I gathered so. I don't know if there's anyone else in the Fellowship rich enough to acquire it? What about that American woman you seemed so matey with?"

He had turned once again to Charlie, about whom he had seemed distinctly uncertain throughout the interview.

"I think she regards the Sneddons with something less than idolatry," said Charlie. Randolph Sneddon laughed.

"I find it difficult to think in terms of 'the Sneddons' at all."

They smiled, got up, made the right noises and took their leave. But even as he walked to the car Charlie was thinking: there was something not quite right about all that. Was it something missing, something wrong, or something that simply hadn't jelled with what they already knew?

Chapter 14

Mother and Son

Charlie Peace spent the night at home in Brixton. He hadn't seen his mother for six months, and was pleased to find that she was without a man. Mrs Peace had been a bad picker of men all her life, and she had finally decided to give up picking. After his experiences of the long string of losers who had shared her life — losers of every race and creed, of every size and shape and every variety of hopelessness — Charlie trusted she could now settle down to a life of single blessedness. When he found she was conceiving a compulsive interest in his love life and marriage prospects he told her bluntly that there was no way such a bad picker as she was was going to be allowed to start picking for him.

Really they got on very well together.

The next morning he was picked up by

Mike Oddie and they began the drive in the direction of Bromley. As they made their stop-go way through suburb after suburb, litter-ridden and burdened with estate agents' signs, Charlie wondered how he had ever borne living in a city which it was so impossible to get out of. He had never felt claustrophobic in London before, but he felt it now. Bromley of course was a cut above most of the places he had driven through, and it soon became clear that they were heading for the better part of Bromley. This was stockbroker's Tudor of the most impressive kind: the houses were bigger, and the artificial beams better fastened to the walls.

"Money," said Charlie.

"A nice class of person," said Oddie.

The Charltons' house, when they found it, was very substantial by commuter-belt standards: set well back, guarded, like the house in Ilkley, by dark evergreens, but giving off a sense of prosperity and well-being. But if the house exuded middle-class doing-very-nicely-thank-you, the woman who opened the heavy front door dissipated that atmosphere more than somewhat.

"You'll be the policemen," she said, with an unconstrainedly friendly smile. "Come along through."

She was in her early thirties, still pretty in a youthful way, and with a figure that eyes had to follow appreciatively. Her sensible skirt and cream blouse were good, but not ostentatiously so, and she wore flat-heeled shoes and no jewellery. The furniture in the large, surprisingly light drawing room was 'thirties-inherited: substantial, well-stuffed and worn. Where the walls were free of radiators there were bookcases — books everywhere, of every conceivable type, from the collector's item to the latest novel in paperback. These were seriously bookish people, as opposed to the bookish dilettante that they had sensed in Suzman's flat.

Coffee cups were set out on a low table, and she went straight into the kitchen and brought in the coffee pot.

"I reckoned on your being on time," she said. "I do like people who are. I'm Virginia Charlton, by the way."

"I'm Detective Superintendent Oddie, and this is Detective Constable Peace. We're both with the West Yorkshire CID."

She smiled sadly and blinked.

"It seems so odd for poor Gerald's murder to be investigated by Yorkshire policemen," she said, sitting down and handing round cups and the sugar bowl. "Sorry — I didn't mean that to sound rude. But he was such a metropolitan person: he loved his clubs, revelled in Soho, liked to be seen at the opera — Covent Garden for preference. If he'd been more of the 'great and good' kind, he'd have sat on governing bodies and Arts Council enquiries."

"But he wasn't?"

"Well, hardly. In fact, not at all. And the great and good don't get themselves murdered, do they? Except casually, and maybe domestically."

"I've known pillars of the community with more secret lives than Walter Mitty," observed Oddie. "But as you say, Gerald Suzman was in any case not one of them. I presume, since he was godfather to your son, that you've known him for some time?"

"Oh yes — quite a time. Ten years or so."

"Did you meet him through your husband?"

"No, though I think Tom has known him longer than me. Tom's been in publishing for twenty-five years. When I met Suzman I was just starting: bottle-washing, humping parcels, running errands. It was my way into the business. Nowadays, with Jonathan growing up, I don't do much more than a bit of copy-editing, but before long I'll be back into publishing — and I was on my way up when I married Tom."

"You haven't told us yet how you and Suzman met."

"I was getting to that. I was doing a stint as stand-in receptionist at Cowper-Hollins, where I worked — where Tom still works — and Gerald came in for an appointment. There was a bit of delay — meeting running over time — and instead of sitting in a chair and browsing through one of our books as most people did, he sat himself on my desk and chatted about me, my prospects, publishing in general. The phrase we'd have used then was that he was 'chatting me up'. I expect there's another, more brutal phrase for it these days."

"But you didn't find it objectionable?"

"No, why should I? I can take care of myself. I thought he was a rather distinguished gentleman."

"You can't remember what his business was?"

"Good heavens, no. I don't suppose I knew at the time."

"Was he a frequent visitor to Cowper-Hollins?"

"Occasional. He had interests in certain books, as a sort of consultant. When I'd got a bit further up the slippery pole I got a better idea what those were."

"What were they?"

"Quite various, really. He was very good on pictures — old engravings, photographs, that kind of thing — so he was often consulted on the illustrations for books, particularly when the author of the book was not very interested. And then there were books with a bibliographical slant: he was very often the outside reader for them at that time, though publishers became a bit more careful later on. Tom may know a bit more about that, though it's not his field."

"Did you or your husband ever hear — rumours?"

"Yes, now and again. If there was anything dubious in his career there would be bound to be whisperings in the publishing world."

"But that didn't put an end to your husband's friendship with him?"

"Oh no. I think Tom regarded him rather as a merchant seaman might regard a pirate: with a sort of disapproving admiration. Tom is rather scholarly, precise, conscientious — a bit of a fish out of water in present-day publishing, or at least a throw-back. You could say that there was an attraction of opposites."

"You never had any specific knowledge of anything he'd done that was dubiously legal?"

"Never. That wasn't my interest. I was looking for good new novelists, and Tom is mainly on the history side."

"So what sort of a friendship was this?"

"Oh — parties where we met, dining together regularly if infrequently, phone calls whenever anything came up that was of mutual interest."

They were interrupted by the sound of the front door and a call of "Mummy! Mummy!" Flushed, Mrs Charlton started up and a second later a little boy burst into the room half-running, half-hopping, his leg heavily bandaged around the knee. He was followed by a capable-looking black girl, still in her teens.

"Mummy! I was running over to talk to Stephen, and I fell over, and — "

He stopped when he saw the strange men.

"I'm sorry, Mrs Charlton," said the girl. "I left Jonathan at the gate as usual, but I stopped to see that he was all right, and he came this awful cropper when he was running over to his friends, as he said. There was blood and he seemed to be in pain, so I whipped him along to the doctor's. He thinks the kneecap may be lightly dislocated, but he says if we keep him home for a day or two there shouldn't be anything to worry about."

"I don't want to stay home!"

"Thank you, Nicole. I'm busy at the moment — "

"I'll take him into the kitchen and get him something nice to eat. Is there any chocolate cake left in the tin?"

"Yes, one good slice."

"Then I'll try to settle him down to some drawing or painting."

"Not easy," said his mother.

"Not easy. Will you be long?"

"Oh" — she looked at Oddie — "I should think half an hour will do it."

Oddie nodded, and the girl took the little boy by the hand and led him out of the room. When the door had shut and the sounds of Jonathan's shouting had receded down the hall, Charlie spoke for the first time since they had arrived.

"Are you sure that Jonathan is only Gerald Suzman's *god*child?"

There was silence. Then Virginia Charlton started speaking, without any of the confidence she had shown before her son's arrival.

"I don't know what you mean . . . What are you implying?"

Mike Oddie stepped in, looking at her closely.

"Constable Peace saw Mr Suzman while he was alive. I only saw him when he had been battered to death. I think you know very well what he is implying."

There was another silence.

"Is there any need for — ?"

"If this has no bearing on Suzman's murder, there's no reason why anything you tell us should go any further," Oddie said. "No promises, but we do always try to handle this sort of thing as discreetly as possible."

Mrs Charlton took a deep breath, then got up and started prowling around the room.

"I haven't been entirely honest."

"No."

"Why does one start talking in clichés at times like this?"

"I don't know, but everybody does."

"That's what clichés are — what everybody says. Well, here goes. I don't see that there is any relevance, but the first meeting was as I told you, but it led to others. He came to Cowper-Hollins several times in the next few weeks, and always tried to bump into me. Eventually I agreed to go out to dinner with him."

"Why? He was well out of your age group.

Did you think he could help you to get ahead in publishing?"

"Oh no. He wasn't *in* publishing at all, in any real sense. No, I'm just attracted to older men. My husband is seventeen years older than me. I suppose people would say I'm looking for father figures. I found boys of my own age callow and brash."

"You must have known what he was after."

"What an old-fashioned phrase! Of course I knew what he was after! It was what I was after too."

"You had an affair?"

"Yes. Well, that's perhaps too definite a word. We slept together now and again. No — that's the wrong word too. Gerald hardly needed any sleep. Most of the time he'd prowl around the flat in his dressing-gown, and not come back to me till it was nearly light. What usually happened was, he would phone and suggest something — a meal, Covent Garden, a party he'd been invited to and I'd go along if it suited, knowing it meant bed afterwards. Mostly it suited."

"Did you get any idea about his professional activities?"

"None. You have to believe me on that. What I told you earlier was true: beyond rumours I knew nothing. I wasn't interested.

I just found the man attractive: clever, subtle, amusing."

"But not a man to marry?"

She shook her head emphatically.

"Oh no! No question of that! And then I started doing real publishing work, then Tom started noticing me and I him, and he *was* a man to marry — gentle, civilised, considerate — and that was the end of Suzman and me. I suppose the truth is that the father-figure I married had to be a *reliable* one. Anyway, as I say, Gerald Suzman became a figure of the past as far as I was concerned."

"For the moment."

She sat down facing them again, her handsome face troubled.

"Yes . . . I'm not at all proud of what happened, and it's difficult to tell you about it . . . We'd been married about two years. Tom had to go to America about a block-buster biography: the sex life of the last Kaiser. Tom thought that historically speaking it was a lot of baloney, but there was every indication it was going to go down big over there. He was going to be away about ten days. Coincidentally I was working on a mystery novel by one of our crime names, one of the ones that gets televised. The book happened to concern the lost Byron memoirs. There was something in it — I forget what it was now — that didn't quite gel, and I rang up Gerald to check. He . . . well, I suspect he could have answered my question off the cuff, but he made a bigger thing out of it, said he had to check several books, said he was coming round to Cowper-Hollins anyway . . . If he'd asked me out to dinner there and then I'd have said no, but the next day he was there at the office and — well, I don't need to go into detail about what happened. He could be very persuasive . . . I have to say that at one point the thought flashed through my mind that Tom and I had been married for two years and the child we'd both wanted had not come along, and if . . . Oh, it's all pretty sordid, or at least morally dubious."

She shook her head, very unhappy with herself.

"But that's in fact how it turned out. And your husband accepted the child as his all along?"

"Oh yes: there's been no problem about that — or at least any problem there is is mine: *I* see, even if he doesn't."

"Wasn't it a bit unwise to choose Gerald Suzman as Jonathan's godfather?"

"It didn't seem so at the time. Tom, you see, is vehemently anti-religion — irrationally so. His mother was converted by the Plymouth Brethren when he was in his teens, and he's always felt that he lost her, that he could never have any sort of relationship with her after that, could hardly even talk to her. I was brought up a high Anglican, and I'm still what you might call an Easter communicant. When I said I'd like Jonathan to be christened, Tom just said 'Fine, so long as I don't have to have anything to do with it.' So I asked the only other Anglo-Catholic I knew to stand godfather, and that was Gerald. We went off one morning to a church in Pimlico and 'had it done.' "

"Did Suzman know he was the father?" Charlie asked.

Virginia Charlton smiled in remembrance.

"Let's say he looked at him closely. At the time Jonathan just looked like a baby — any baby. But Suzman met us some time later, when Jon was about three, in Selfridges during the Christmas bun-fight. He took him up in his arms and talked to him and, well, by then the resemblance was becoming more marked. I'm sure he saw what you saw — in fact I know he did, because he looked at me roguishly and winked. I expect it was around that time that he made the will in his favour."

"Did you know that he had?"

Virginia Charlton hesitated for a moment.

"We met at a party, nearly a year ago . . . He got me into a corner, well away from Tom, and said that when he, Gerald, died, which he wasn't intending to do for a long time yet, Jonathan would be the gainer. But he hoped to see something of the boy when he was grown up . . . I shouldn't be admitting this, should I?"

"It's always better to tell the truth rather than having it prised out of you," said Oddie. "What did you say?"

"I said in the meanwhile keep well away. That sounds pretty ungrateful, but he was sophisticated and sensible about it. He realised I didn't want him seen *with* Jonathan, so that the resemblance could be noted. In particular I didn't want them together when Tom was around."

"Did he tell you how much his estate was likely to amount to?"

"No. How could he know, anyway? His business was a pretty dodgy one, with plenty of ups and downs. He said something like: 'It won't be riches, dear girl, but it'll be something for the proverbial rainy day, if he turns out to be the dreary sort of person who is always expecting one.' I'd bet on a few thousand."

"I think rather more than that," said Oddie,

getting up and gesturing to Charlie to do the same. "Well, I think that covers most things. I'm sure you must see that this does give you an interest in his death. May I ask what you were doing on Sunday evening?"

"Of course. I knew you'd ask that. We had a small dinner-party here."

And she named a writing couple with such stupendously right-thinking credentials that they had supported every good radical cause going in the last quarter-century and as a consequence had the distinction of never having appeared in any Honours List. And she gave them their address and telephone number to boot. Oddie smiled briefly.

"That does sound like rather a splendid alibi. Tell me, how did your husband react to Suzman's death?"

"He said that if he *had* to go now, that might be the way he would have chosen: mysterious, sensational — not *ordinary*."

"And you're not afraid that one day he might look at Jonathan and *wonder?*"

"Fortunately Tom is very short-sighted," said his wife.

Chapter 15

Lighten Our Darkness

"I think we should split up," said Mike Oddie, as they stood in the forecourt of a horrible hamburger joint, eating horrible hamburgers. "I think we should get the message back to Batley Bridge that operations are going to shift back to West Yorkshire. There are a lot of people we need to talk to again up there, and we don't want those that remain simply to evaporate. I'll ring up the operations room at the Cumberland, and they can give a message to the landlord."

"I'll ring up my b. and b.," said Charlie. "That'll get it round the place. And maybe Lettie as well."

"That Norwegian girl staying up at Micklewike wasn't leaving till Friday, was she?"

"No, but I'm not so sure about Vidkun Whatsit. I think he may already have gone.

By the way, one person we haven't interviewed is Felicity Coggenhoe."

"Do it. Give yourself a treat. Take the train, talk to her in Leeds, pick up the photocopies from Ilkley, then try to be back in Batley Bridge by this evening."

"Sounds good. What are you going to do?"

"Someone's got to talk to the other bookshop manager. Seems silly for both of us to waste our time. Then I thought I'd go back to the Yard and see if they've picked up anything new since yesterday."

"I knew you were jealous of my Yard connections. You're trying to get a foot in that door."

"I might be jealous if I had any desire to live in this Godforsaken part of the country. Still, I would like to have another talk with your Mr Trethowan if he's free. It was him that set us on to Suzman in the first place. I'd like to know if they've got anything concrete on Suzman's financial standing."

"Well, while you mull over the bank statements I'll mull over the Sneddon letters," said Charlie. "It seems a fair swap." They threw away a half of their hamburgers and made towards the car. "I've got my things in the back. Leave me at the nearest

Underground station and I'll get back up North."

It took Mike Oddie quite a time to drive to Pocklington. The drive took him through landscape and townscapes very different from what he was used to: gentle slopes predominated in the terrain, and tweeness and genteelery in the buildings, though there were small signs here and there that where once everyone had been well-heeled, now the heels were wearing down. Mike Oddie tried to suppress a feeling of satisfaction that, whereas the last recession had bludgeoned mainly the North, this time it was hitting the South as well. He tried, but he failed.

He found Pocklington nestling, as villages of that sort are always said to do, in the Sussex Downs. It was overpoweringly middle-class and picture-postcard, more a location for a TV crime series than a real place. It was difficult to believe that the pub could sell anything so vulgar as beer. The shops did not sell meat or fish but designer clothes, antiques, or souvenirs. Suzman's, the anti-quarian second-hand booksellers, fitted in very well: it was recently painted, bright as a new pin, and its shelves were groaning with leather-bound desirables from the li-braries of gentlefolk.

It was a very different figure who rose to

greet him from the manager of the Piccadilly store: long, fair locks falling over his eyes, baggy sports-jacket and flannel trousers, and a general air of enthusiasm and youth. It was possible he even loved books.

"Oh, police. I wondered if you'd be calling here. I'm Simon Westbury, by the way: manager, one-man band, general dogsbody. Do you want me to close the shop? We do most of our business by post, so it's not likely we'll be disturbed."

"Don't bother, then. You say you wondered whether we'd be on to you?"

The man gave him an attractive, lop-sided grin.

"Well — murder, with literary connections, generally bookish in some way. I thought if there wasn't any obvious motive — sexual, say, or financial — that you might be looking at that side of his life. I must say I always wondered about that Micklewike Weekend."

"In what way?"

"Well, there had to be *some*thing, didn't there?"

"Why? Because there always was with him?"

Simon Westbury thought.

"No. That's almost but not quite true. Suzman had a part of him that genuinely

237

loved books. This bookshop is an expression of that part. He almost never put anything dodgy through this shop. You'll say I would say that, but it happens to be true. The books he loved and sold here were mainly the nineteenth century ones which are our speciality: the novelists, the poets, even the hack dramatists that came before Shaw. Our real interests went up to, say, Wells and Galsworthy in the fiction line, but not beyond. Now, Susannah Sneddon was very much a figure of the 'twenties. And that heavy-breathing-in-the-hedgerow stuff was laughably outside Gerald's natural interests. Ergo, I was always convinced that his attraction to her sprang from the other side of him."

"The crooked side?"

"Exactly."

"And did you work out what precisely was crooked about the whole enterprise?"

He shook his head with an engaging candour.

"No, I never did. I'm looking forward to you finding that out. Very interesting."

"How much did you discuss it with him?"

"Not greatly. It's outside my own sphere of interest too."

"You didn't even speculate in your own mind?"

He pursed his lips.

"I suppose I did. If it had been an author who was popular with the rich and influential — Trollope, say, or Waugh — then I'd say that readers, the members of the new Fellowship, were the target. It would be in character for him to see them as targets, either for getting money out of them, or as important contacts. But that's not Susannah Sneddon's audience at all: in spite of the feminist interest in her these days, her appeal was and is basically middle-class, middle-brow, with a reasonably strong appeal to the young. Not at all the sort of people whom Suzman usually cultivated. So as I say the whole thing was a mystery to me, and one I've never solved."

"Did Suzman ever talk to you about his . . . dodgier enterprises?"

"Not directly. Not in so many words. This, and the West End shop, were his impeccable fronts to the world, so he wouldn't have. But if he was talking about his various interests, things sometimes slipped out that made me think this or that might be dubious — particularly if he 'purred' as I always called it to myself: gave off a feeling of being particularly pleased with himself."

"Anything of that kind recently?"

"Oh, there were always one or two things of that kind in the pipeline. I do remember his saying a week or two ago that he was going to meet a Norwegian up in Micklewike — about a Knut Hamsun letter. He was purring a good deal about that, so I would think there was something very fishy there."

Mike Oddie sighed with satisfaction. At last the bland exterior of Vidkun Mjølhus was going to get some detail added to it. He had not been there for love of Susannah Sneddon.

"Now that is interesting. Who is this Knut Hamsun? Is there any interest in him in this country?"

"Oh yes, of a cult kind. Quite a lot more in the States, with its big Scandinavian population. He's a very fine writer. And there's one more thing about him: he was a Nazi sympathiser."

"Ah!"

"During the German occupation of Norway he was an apologist for the Quisling government. Not a popular stand to take, not then, nor after the war, when he stood by it and was put in an asylum. But he had always had a strong streak of obstinacy, and by then he was a cussed old sod. Suzman told me that the letter was a late one, written a year or two before his death, defending his stand. That could be the reason for his interest."

That surprised Oddie.

"Why? Suzman wasn't a right-wing nutter, was he?"

"Hardly. Almost a-political, I would say. No, I mean that it would increase its value commercially. Think of all the extreme right-wing, neo-Fascist groups springing up all over Europe, East and West. Think of the shops and dealers specialising in Nazi memorabilia. Most of it is junk for the skinheads, but there is a more cultivated — no, that's the wrong word — a more affluent interest in the Fascist regimes of the 'thirties and 'forties as well. A letter of that sort could be very saleable."

"Do you think it was a genuine letter?"

"In view of the purring I'd say not."

"It seems an odd departure for him — like the Sneddon business, in fact."

"No, it's not really. Hamsun lived a very long time. His early books are late nineteenth century, well within our field of interest. And there's another thing."

"Yes?"

"People — the police, and literary experts — are getting very sophisticated about forgeries in this country. The scope is much more limited than it was."

"I rather suspected that, from what they told me at Haworth Parsonage."

241

"That's right. They've suffered from literary shysters there. Well, Norway is a small, rather out-of-the-way country. Not backward, but backward in the sophistications of literary chicanery and its detection. No significant experience of it. Then again, they have plenty of fine writers and one great one — or many would argue two: Ibsen and Hamsun. No, my bet is that this was a broadening out, a development of a line which had become blocked for him, at least to a degree, here in this country: out and out forgery."

"For which, obviously, he'd need a Norwegian accomplice."

"Almost certainly."

"It could be I know who that is," said Oddie.

Felicity Coggenhoe had a bedsitter in — inevitably — Headingly. When Charlie got back to Leeds in the early evening he collected a car from the pool at Police Headquarters and went straight there. It was a comfortless room, suggesting no great parental generosity, but she had made it personal with posters and rugs. She was writing an essay against a deadline on a rather rickety table set to catch the evening sun, but she offered him a mug of instant coffee with powdered milk, and he accepted. She seemed extremely pleased to see him.

"I've heard all about you from my parents, who've been making agitated phone calls from Batley Bridge. They say they were 'deceived' in you, but even they admit that maybe you did it in the course of your job."

"I'm surprised to hear they admit that."

"Oh, it was never a colour thing. How is the investigation going?"

"Progressing in a hundred directions. I'm not really allowed to talk about it. Are your parents still in Batley Bridge?"

"They were due to go home today — 'with the future of the Sneddon Fellowship assured,' as my father informed me last night. I suppose that means it's all sewn up that he's going to be in charge. He also said that they'd been deluged with enquiries about membership."

"That figures. Murder does attract all sorts of weirdos," said Charlie.

"All those people wanting a share in the Sneddons, and now hundreds more wanting a tiny part in the Suzman murder."

"Like vultures hovering," said Charlie, remembering his earlier impressions. "Including your parents of course." Felicity grinned her agreement. "Do you know how much contact they had with Suzman before they came to Batley Bridge?"

"I only know what they told me. I suppose you've asked them? Oh, I see — you don't necessarily believe them. Fair enough. All I know is that my father said he'd talked on the phone to Gerald Suzman before the Weekend."

"And at the Weekend?"

"Well, as you know, during the Weekend if I wasn't with them I was with you. Whilst I was with them the contacts between them and Mr Suzman were of the most innocuous kind. Just casual social encounters. While I was with you, who knows? I had the impression that they spent their time steaming around trying to find out where their chick had escaped to, but that may be just my paranoia. They may have been having meetings or making telephone calls I knew nothing about."

"By the way," said Charlie, curious, "you said just now their attitude to me had nothing to do with colour. What did it have to do with?"

Felicity looked down.

"I'm afraid it was drugs. I was expelled from my private school when I was sixteen for experimenting with drugs. I shouldn't have said it was *nothing* to do with colour.

I'm afraid they associate black people with drugs."

"Charming."

"I'm deeply ashamed."

"For experimenting with drugs?"

"For them and their prejudices, you oaf! They assumed I was back in the drugs scene, just because I was going around with you. It was very unintelligent. In fact the drugs *were* only an experiment, springing from a general feeling of being underloved and irrelevant. My mother's life revolves around my father, and so does my father's. His greatest pleasure is saying 'As a writer myself,' and hers is saying 'My husband, the writer.' It's never left much room for me."

"I got the idea at one point that their concern for you was really a concern for themselves and their image."

"Your idea is right. Dad can't be said to have an image at the moment, but he's pulling out all stops to get one."

"But the drugs business is over?"

"Over? Long ago. I'm happy here, have friends, am doing quite well, and thinking towards going on to do a Ph.D."

"Another opus on the rural novels of you-know-who?"

She gave him a rueful smile.

"We-e-ell . . . I *was* thinking of doing

D. H. Lawrence. A really feminist diatribe on the *awfulness* of the man and his attitudes and most of what he wrote. With the re-establishment of the copyright and the new, unexpurgated texts there's a wealth of new material, most of it damning. But with all this coming up, I have toyed with the idea of Susannah Sneddon, Mary Webb and one or two more. I'd treat them as popular writers, of course, and not make exaggerated claims, but I could tie them in with D. H. Lawrence, and maybe bring in Winifred Holtby, though she didn't really write grunting-on-the-stable-floor stuff. It is a thought, though . . ."

"I found I got a bit fed up with Susannah Sneddon by the third book I read."

"Oh, I'd probably find the same. By the time I have to decide on a subject I'll probably have gone off on to an entirely new tack: Elizabethan drama or Romantic poetry or something major and mainstream. I might not be willing to settle for a back-alley of literature. God knows, I've had enough second-rate fiction in my life!"

"Well," said Charlie, getting up from the bed on which he had been sitting and making notes. "I'm off to Ilkley, then back to Batley Bridge."

"Ilkley?" Her eyes lit up with an excitement that had a hint of voracity in it. "Is that the Sneddon letters people? Are you going to read the letters?"

"I am. You're obviously not all that fed up with second-rate fiction writers."

"It *would* be interesting."

"Can't take you along, I'm afraid. But we are hoping to get together with a few of the Weekend people tomorrow — those who are still around. Follow up some of the things they said in their initial statements. Any chance of your coming over to Batley Bridge?"

"I've got two lectures early on, and I've got to hand this essay in. I could be over there by lunchtime, or not much later."

"It's not quite the first date I had in mind, but it'll do," said Charlie, bending and kissing her on the cheek, then raising his hand in farewell.

Mike Oddie had pulled into a motel on the A1. It was not far out of London, but it gave him the basis for an early start in the morning. He had showered, poured himself a small Scotch from the emergency flask that he always had with him and added plenty of water. Then he lay on his back thinking about what he had learnt.

Charlie's friend at Scotland Yard, Superintendent Trethowan, had dug up some pretty interesting new stuff about Suzman's recent activities. He had not entirely given up on the forgeries, apparently. There had been an obscene early short story by Joe Orton, snapped up eagerly by a collector in Chelsea from a dealer known to be a friend of Suzman's. The paper it had been written on certainly dated from the 'fifties, but the state of the typewriter was identical with its condition when Orton was writing *What the Butler Saw* at the end of his life a decade later. The piece was hastily reclassified as a late one, possibly by Orton's friend Halliwell. Almost certainly, though the collector was not inclined to accept this, the piece was a forgery: somehow Suzman had got hold of Orton's typewriter, and had put together a scatological piece in the pair's early manner — much easier to imitate than the epigrammatic demotic of Orton's mature plays. Money in the bank for Suzman, yet he was never directly associated with the typescript.

And so it went on: dodgy hitherto-unknown private printings of short pieces, unknown early manuscript versions of well-known poems with interesting variant readings, doctored first editions. All of them meaning a nice little cash sum for Gerald

Suzman, but none of them being directly traceable back to him. He had perfected his art as a sort of literary Houdini. Oddie guessed that some of the pleasure, for him, lay in the sheer cleverness of the operation: it was an optional extra to the money.

But money there undoubtedly was. The information collected by Scotland Yard gave an idea of wealth that was, if not staggering, then extremely impressive: leaving aside his flat and his two businesses, all lightly mortgaged, his various bank accounts, building society accounts and investments amounted to some three hundred thousand. There was also the Micklewike farm which Oddie rather suspected might have been sold when agricultural property picked up, and when it had served its turn. And he was willing to bet there were assets stashed away abroad.

So the answer to the question of *cui bono?* was that Jonathan Charlton benefitted considerably, and so, more indirectly, did his parents. But that dinner-party alibi was hard to break. The impeccably credentialled writing pair had unanimously assured him on the phone that they had been with the Charltons in Bromley until eleven o'clock. Somehow he could not regard the Charltons — though admittedly he had not met the husband — as likely murderers. Did the murder bear the hallmark less of murder for gain than of a falling-out of thieves? He rather thought it did. And if so the Norwegian began to come more clearly into focus. Was the whole Sneddon business — whatever the crooked plan behind it, and Oddie was in no doubt that there was one — merely a red herring, or perhaps a smoke-screen?

But as he lay there sipping his drink he remained convinced that the question of who benefitted was central to the riddle of who took Suzman's life: it was just that the terms of the question had to be changed, or enlarged, or made less basic. But for the life of him he couldn't think how.

Charlie collected the photocopies of Susannah Sneddon's letters from the late-duty sergeant in Ilkley.

"I read one or two of them while I was copying them," the sergeant said glumly. "The changing seasons in Micklewike. I wish you joy of them — rather you than me. But there's obviously some as'll find them interesting. People are ringing up the Potter-Hodges about them. I've already had them in to collect their photocopies."

"How did they strike you?"

"Oh, the Potter-Hodges are well-known

in Ilkley. Respected local citizens. They're no oil-painting, I admit. He always reminds me of one of those listed houses that the owner is letting go to rack and ruin so he can demolish and sell the land for development. Still, it's not everyone can be handsome young fellows like thee an' me, is it?"

He winked. He was a good forty-five, and homely.

Charlie had rung the Ludlums from London to advise them of his return, but when he got to Batley Bridge he first slipped in to the Duke of Cumberland and went to the little operations centre set up there. He read through various messages from Mike Oddie, and put in train a request to the Oslo police for any information they could dig up on Vidkun Mjølhus. Then he went down to the bar for a pint, less from any need of one than from a desire to advertise the fact that enquiries had shifted back to the Batley Bridge area. He was received with enthusiasm by the landlord, avid delight by Lettie, and an interest everywhere. It is not often, these days, that policemen find themselves so popular.

"What have you found out about Suzman?" whispered Lettie, when he had settled down at her table in the Saloon Bar. "Have

251

you found out what was behind this Weekend?"

"I can't tell you what we've found out about Suzman," Charlie replied, his voice equally low. "But I think I can say we still don't know what was behind the Sneddon Fellowship."

"I've been to see my mother again," Lettie said. "She's beginning to get very crabby and complains that I'm asking questions about the Sneddons the whole time. All she wants to talk about is her hard life. I can't think of a subject I'm less interested in. I don't think I'll be going again, unless you have something specific you want me to get from her. She asked me last time when I was coming back here to live. Next time she'll be assuming I'll have her to live with me!"

Back in his bed and breakfast place, where he parried questions with the assurance that they could have a good chat over breakfast, Charlie bathed, set out his things, then walked around the room thinking over his day. Then in his little notebook he made the entry: "needed little sleep." After a pause for thought he added another one: "copyright?"

Then he turned on his bedside light, got into bed, and settled down to read the letters of Susannah Sneddon.

Chapter 16

Letters

The letters spanned thirteen years. They were reasonably regular — every three or four months — and were meticulously dated. The sergeant at the Ilkley police station had helpfully put them into chronological order. They were beautifully written, and the early ones showed a self-consciousness of style such as many fledgling authors display. Susannah Sneddon was trying her wings as a writer:

"Now, with the coming of Spring, I feel the earth tremulously stirring into life, with tiny blades and shoots of hope and promise bravely piercing the soil, even here in exposed, windswept Micklewike. Yet the other day I was walking past the open door of the barn and I heard the wind sweeping up the dead leaves inside and dashing them against the walls, so that the whole building seemed alive, the leaves resuscitated in a monstrous dance of death. When I think of our nation, slowly returning to life after the four dreadful years of slaughter, I see that same mingling of the dead and the living, see the timid shoots of new life peering up from the graves of our dead sons . . ."

That was in 1919, when the series of letters began. Charlie frowned a little at the tone: she was very hot on natural observation, was our Susannah. She wrote about hawthorn and bluebells as if they were never to be seen in distant Ilkley: "I know how you too once felt the rhythms of the seasons, the tug of Spring and the sated relaxation of Autumn," she wrote to her friend at one stage. There seemed to be an undertone of pity, even of contempt, for the friend who had left Micklewike to marry an urban grocer.

Quite early on there were hints of her ambitions: "Oh, if only I could give shape to my feelings — give them *form,* find characters who could experience them, embody them." And later:

"Joshua is writing, strange, disordered

stuff, sitting at his old table in snatched moments in the evenings. He does not talk about it, but I read it when I am alone in the day, and do not understand it. That is not the sort of writing that I crave to do, but then I do not have the experience of having been in the trenches. He does not talk about that either, but I know that it is with him every hour of the day, haunting him."

And then, in the summer of 1920, it became explicit: "I am writing a novel!"

With experience of her writing and style it became easy for Charlie to skip the passages of fine writing. There was a mixture of self-indulgence and showing-off about them that he found distasteful. In any case they became less frequent as Susannah had her fiction into which to channel them. More interesting to him were the glimpses of life at High Maddox Farm, and the progress of the pair's careers as writers:

"My novel has been accepted! Carter and Foreman have taken it, and think it will do modestly well! I am to get money for it, what they call an advance! The delight of this is beyond anything I can describe — it warms my whole body, gives dance to every step I take.

"Picture us, if you will, of an evening, Joshua at his little table, I at mine, two pools of light in the darkening room, he penning the tormented gaieties of his strange novel, I trying to encompass the dark feel of the earth, the heartstopping joy of the thrust of Spring. Yes, I am writing a second novel — how could I not, in the drunken enthusiasm of being now a soon-to-be-published writer? The first is called *Orchard's End*, and the new one *Between the Furrows*. Oh, the joy, Janet, of being a writer! Nothing will touch me now — not our poverty, our hunger, the hardness of our lives. And perhaps it will not be so hard for us in future. They are paying me fifty pounds!!!!"

Inevitably Charlie was interested in the woman's love-affair, if such there had been. There was an early reference to "Hugh." Susannah was talking about her hatred of "the everyday — of cooking and cleaning, washing and mending, shopping and gossiping," and she added: "perhaps if things had been different with Hugh I would go about them contentedly. But perhaps not." That last sentence suggested to Charlie a welcome douche of realism and self-knowledge.

Then much later, at the time she was writing *The Barren Fields* and was having trouble over "a very passionate scene," she confessed: "if only Hugh and I had been *more* to each other, if there had been something beyond yearning looks and fleeting touches, for what we had was a love that could never put itself into words." That seemed odd and ambiguous to Charlie: he began to wonder not only if the affair had been completely chaste — that had always been a possibility — but if it had been more in Susannah's imagination than a thing of the real world: yearning looks and fleeting touches are very easy to imagine. Then he considered another possibility: Susannah was after all a novelist, and could be trying to convey a totally false impression to her friend. In 1930 she wrote: "Hugh's wife died last week. I felt nothing, nothing at all. That was another era, another life, it happened to another person. I am a writer. I live in my books." The words put Charlie uncomfortably in mind of Rupert Coggenhoe.

Joshua was much more frequently mentioned than the shadowy Hugh. At one point she said: "They despise him in the village because he is a poor farmer, who has ambitions beyond the everyday. They have no mercy, no vision: they cannot see that the sordid business of scraping a wretched living clings like sticky mud, prevents the soul soaring." When his first book — she said she couldn't think of them as novels, because there was no story, hardly any characters you could identify as such — was published, to universal apathy, she recorded him as smiling grimly, and then going about his farm work as usual.

Work was really what clung to Joshua in these letters: ploughing, hoeing, feeding, sowing, harvesting — the mentions of this round of farm activities were off-hand, but somehow there came through a feeling of unremitting, backbreaking toil, such as the modern world hardly knows. And then, in the evenings, often into the night, there he was at his little table, lit at first by gas lamp, only later by electricity, struggling at those books that nobody wanted to read. From the letters he did not get the impression that Joshua was of the "every sentence is a torture" school of writers, but rather that he wrote and discarded, rewrote and rediscarded. And when further books came out, to further apathy, there were further grim smiles. The most Susannah recorded him as saying was "Maybe their time will come."

He certainly read Susannah's novels. There

was a moment of comedy when "Cousin George from over Abbothall way" paid them a visit to protest about Susannah writing "mucky stories," and claimed that she was bringing the Sneddon name into disrepute. Joshua stood up for his sister, and said that any farmer who couldn't stand a bit of copulation shouldn't be in the livestock business. Cousin George's stock in trades were business efficiency allied with narrow religion. His great delight seemed to be in coming over to give Joshua good advice of the "they turnips will never thrive" kind. Charlie remembered a character in *The Black Byre* of that type: a mean-spirited and grasping petty tyrant. He rather suspected he was here meeting the original of that character. Joshua, at any rate, took little notice of him. "That'll give Cousin George something to rail about," he would say, in the wake of any minor farm disaster. All disasters seemed to rouse in him the stoicism of one who had known life in the trenches of the First World War, one to whom nothing worse could happen. But his generosity had not been killed with his hope. When Susannah recorded herself reading to him one of her hotter scenes, his reaction was similar to that to his farming setbacks: "That'll make Cousin George sweat!"

It was clear enough from the letters that Joshua was a poor and a reluctant farmer, and that the money from Susannah's books came in very welcome for the household from time to time. Not that she poured it into the farm, or handed it over to Joshua in the way some Victorian literary ladies are said to have handed their earnings over to their husbands. But there were references in the letters to Susannah handing over money on occasion to Joshua for specific agricultural purposes — the purchase of seed, or of new implements. "This is my home, my land," she wrote to her friend. "If I must pay to keep it, I will pay." She made no references to Joshua's jealousy of her success, but she did record that he did not like her books greatly. "Life's not like that," he said when he had read *The Barren Fields*. "It doesn't progress, go forwards, have beginnings and endings. It just jolts along messily." There spoke once more, perhaps, the man of the trenches.

Susannah said little to her friend about money. She might casually mention advances — one hundred pounds, apparently, for *The Barren Fields* and fifty more for the novels which succeeded it. They seemed to earn their advances and more, because twice a year there were mentions of royalties ("those are the monies which the books have earned, Janet dear"), and occasionally the expression of pleasure at the size of the cheque: "*Very* happy with my royalties, pleased with my publishers. There is talk of a cheap edition." But what really intoxicated her was the joy of writing, of being published, from time to time of getting letters from her readers: "To give pleasure is to have a feeling of great power — and great joy!"

Susannah recorded in many of her letters the walks she took while planning a new chapter: the views over the Yorkshire countryside, the farmyard sights and smells, the creatures in the hedgerows. And then: "to sit down, gratefully, and for the words to flow, the people to come alive, the landscape to glow and shimmer on paper." Then she was in a world of her own, and Charlie could well imagine that she hated interruptions: "This morning I was deep in the complexities of a first chapter when Mrs Blatchley arrived with her dough-faced daughter. I had forgotten it was Thursday, her day. The chapter shattered — fell apart around me. Tomorrow I must take a long, long walk to try to put it together again."

She was very conscious that she had the day to write in whereas her brother had only snatched moments at night. When they acquired a wireless set in 1931 she said she was careful never to switch it on when he was working. She was rather contemptuous of it anyway: "such a poor alternative to peace and quiet."

All this time Susannah and Joshua were in and of Micklewike: not loved by the villagers, nor loving them, but constantly there, utterly rooted, in a grudging way accepted. In all the years before 1930 covered by the letters Charlie found reference only to one visit to Ilkley to see her friend, when she came home the same evening, and one to Leeds for dental work that could not be done closer to home. She had hated the place. "The traffic and the noise, and the smells and the constant bustle and barging of the people — everything combined to give me my sharpest anticipation yet of Hell itself!" She had gone straight from the station to the dental surgeon, then straight back to the station. She had used the comparative wealth from the books to pay: "Ten pounds! But the joy of being no longer distracted from work by a dull ache in the mouth makes it worthwhile."

Then in 1930 she was asked down to London by her publishers. As far as Charlie could see from the letters this was an act of pure kindness on their part. Susannah mentioned to her friend no good business reason for the trip, only that Walter Allemby at Carter and Foreman would like to meet her, having published her with the anticipated modest success and a bit more for several years. He suggested that they book her into a hotel overnight, and that next day she could come to the firm's offices, meet people in charge of the various aspects of publishing, then have lunch and be put on the afternoon train back to Leeds. After some hesitation Susannah agreed. She wrote to her friend that she anticipated no pleasure from the trip, but said that Mr Allemby had always been so kind and helpful that she thought it right to accede to his desire for a meeting. She went down into Batley Bridge to buy a new dress.

The next letter showed that she had been right in anticipating little pleasure. On the long (four hours — who said the railways were better then?) train journey from Leeds to London she was interested in the scenery she passed through, but she thought it "flat and wet," and felt that it was a worthless experience to see nature at such a high speed. Carter and Foreman had booked her into the Great Northern Hotel at King's Cross. Arriving there in the late afternoon she apparently spent the rest of the day skulking in her room, or scuttling to the bathroom and lavatory when the corridors were clear. She seemed absurdly conscious that the hotel staff were laughing at her as a country bumpkin, though of all hotels a railway one must have been most used to a heterogeneous clientele. Susannah seemed to have an infinite capacity to go without food, and she ate neither dinner nor breakfast.

The offices of Carter and Foreman were near Covent Garden, and as the Piccadilly line went there directly from King's Cross Mr Allemby had suggested she take the Underground. The suggestion was certainly well-meant, but unfortunate. Susannah got her ticket, and then was confronted by the recently installed escalator. Too flurried to realize that there were also conventional steps she stood at the top, jostled by the other passengers, trying to summon up the courage to step on to it. When someone swore at her for getting in his way she turned and fled — "out into the hideous roar of traffic, more awful than even I could have contemplated, and into the comparative safety of a taxi."

When she arrived at the offices of Carter and Foreman things began to go better.

"Mr Allemby was very kind, as I knew

he must be. If he noticed that I was flurried he made no comment. He must have registered my provincial appearance, my shabby shoes, my lack of 'face paint', but he never let his eye rest on my deficiencies. He is, after all, a gentleman. His secretary brought us tea and biscuits in his office — most welcome! — and we talked about how well the cheap edition of *The Barren Fields* is doing. To be bought and read by so many ordinary people, people like myself, is a great pleasure. Then the talk ranged around a little — the progress of the new novel, even such restful, uncontroversial topics as punctuation (once my downfall, though no longer). All was calming and peaceful, apart from the dreadful roar of motor vehicles outside, and the calls of the market men. When he thought I was sufficiently refreshed, Mr Allemby took me to the office of Mr Carter, son of the founder of the firm, who was gentle, unworldly and most kind. It was clear that he had read and enjoyed my books!! I had thought that the head of the firm would be a businessman purely, but he was not so: he discussed the books in detail, and told me his preferences. But this was true of all the firm's members to whom I was introduced. They were happy to speak of my books, and all expressed the pleasure they got from them. One of them asked if it took all day to come from Micklewike to Leeds! Another asked if I had access to a telephone in my home village.

Then came the moment I was dreading: lunch. I was to be accompanied by Mr Allemby, Mr Carter and Miss Murchison, who is an accountant, and the only woman in the firm. Mr Allemby said they had thought I would prefer somewhere quiet. (I am sure he meant somewhere not fashionable, somewhere where I would not look *too* out of place!) I nodded dumbly. It was a five-minute walk — I was almost too terrified to cross the road, but Mr Allemby took my arm and guided me though the *madly* careering motor cars and omnibuses. The restaurant was very grand to my eyes (a great deal of plush and gilt), but probably very ordinary to theirs. When I found that the menu was a conventional English one I was so relieved I looked at Mr Allemby gratefully, and he smiled and nodded. I was able to order leek and potato soup, with steak and oyster pie to follow, without any feeling that I would make a fool of myself by not knowing the correct way to eat them.

They tried — for they are all kind people — to make me feel more at home than I really could. I told them shyly that this was the first time in my life I had been to a restaurant. They pressed me that this could not be the truth, but I insisted on it: that I had been twice in a café — once with you, Janet dear! — but never before in a restaurant. To take my mind off my uncertainties they encouraged me to talk about my writing. I tried to tell them of the joy I had in it: not just in creating, but in the lovely business of writing *itself*. Mr Allemby told me, rather hesitantly, perhaps fearful of offending, that I am now the last of their authors to submit handwritten manuscripts."

Charlie, in danger of falling asleep, jerked himself awake. Surely no one at that date would do that? But there it was:

". . . the last of their authors to submit handwritten manuscripts. Mr Allemby complimented me on my beautiful handwriting, and I said I had been very well taught. (Remember Miss Cross — Cross-patch! — and all those rapped knuckles for slovenly penmanship?) Miss Murchison said she had been talking to the firm's printers on the telephone only that day, and the gentleman there said he actually preferred my handwritten manuscripts to many that were done with the typewriter. He said they were 'so beautifully legible' — as great a tribute as Crosspatch can ever have had! I refrained from any sweet course . . ."

Eureka!
The old stone house on the Haworth Road was dark and still, so Charlie could not let out a victory yell. But he punched his fist in the air, in the manner of goal scorers.

But as the significance of the letter sank in he paused in his jubilation. He turned over in his bed, put the photocopies on the bedside table and switched off the lamp. Then he lay on his back, thinking.

The typescript at the farm was a fake. The purple passages in the typescript were inventions. Mr Suzman had been up to his old tricks: he had got a typewriter of the period, and paper, and had put together a fake. There never had been any typescript of a Susannah Sneddon novel.

Before he drifted off into his usual dream-less sleep Charlie registered a definite sense that his discovery raised as many questions as it solved.

Chapter 17

Oxenthorpe Again

The Duke of Cumberland, when Charlie got there next morning, was as much in contrast to its somnolent out-of-season self as it had been every day since the Sneddon Weekend began. Breakfast trade was booming, and extra staff had been laid on. Campers came in, forsaking their own burst bangers on spirit stoves to get the authentic whiff of murder. It was even said that some Batley Bridge locals had taken to breakfasting there, on the feeble excuse that they had forgotten how to do a real, old-fashioned English breakfast.

Charlie told Mike Oddie of his discovery of the night before in the Incident Room.

"It's a whopping, massive *fact*," Oddie said, his forehead creased. "But it doesn't give us a *motive*."

"No, it doesn't," agreed Charlie. "The

typescripts would be worth a fair bit in themselves, though, if they were accepted as genuine. And remember those proofs that arrived on the day he died? There was going to be a new edition of the novels, with all the added steam that Suzman had dreamed up. I imagine he'd get money out of them too."

"I expect he would. How many Sneddon novels were there all together?"

"Twelve, by Susannah. I suppose he'd get some sort of royalty as editor, wouldn't he? Whether it would amount to much for someone of Suzman's financial standing is another matter."

"But it was a standing achieved precisely by frauds of this kind," Oddie pointed out. "Of which we now have another example in a forged Hamsun letter. I must say this does bear all the hallmarks of a falling-out among thieves, and in the case of the letter we have a second thief to look closely at. Is there anything from the Norwegian police yet?"

"Nothing. I did see the Norwegian girl — woman, sorry — lurking around downstairs when I came in just now. I think everyone on the fringes of the case is lurking around the Duke of Cumberland, when they're not up at Micklewike. I wonder if it might be worthwhile having another chat with her?"

There were routine matters to clear up first, and by the time they went in search of her the bars were open. She was sitting over a fruit juice with Gillian Parkin, and the two were on to the inevitable subject of the typescripts. Oddie and Charlie came upon them unnoticed from behind, and stood listening for a moment.

"As far as I can gather from what he said, just the one book was going through press at the moment. Leaving presumably eleven — though I don't recall him ever actually saying he had the typescripts for all twelve. But he did imply there would be a succession of new editions. If we could get permission to edit just one — we could do it jointly — "

"Boy, do we have bad news for you," said Charlie, insensitively. They jumped up as if they had somehow been caught out, then turned questioning faces towards the two policemen.

"I'm afraid the typescripts are forgeries," said Oddie.

They leapt out of their seats.

"No!" they screamed. "I don't believe you."

"They must be real! They read just like her style!"

"And just the look of them . . . ."

"I'm afraid it's the essence of literary forgery that they look right and read right," said Oddie. "Unfortunately they *aren't* right. Suzman had very good reasons for keeping the editing of the new editions in his own hands. Susannah Sneddon never made typescripts, and neither did anyone else. We've established from the letters to her friend in Ilkley that she sent handwritten manuscripts to her publishers, which they then sent straight to the printers."

"I don't believe it!" said Gillian Parkin, though it was clear she did. She sank back into her chair. "Handwritten manuscripts in the 'twenties?"

"It was unusual," put in Charlie. "Her publishers told her she was the last of their authors to do it. But I suppose it was the usual thing — the only thing — up until the last quarter of the nineteenth century."

The two women thought.

"What were the letters like?" asked Gillian Parkin. "Would they be publishable, do you think?"

Charlie repressed the image of wings flapping over carrion that came once again unbidden to his mind. He tried to give a considered reply.

"I thought they were interesting. I didn't

feel I actually liked the woman very much
— "

"Liked!" pounced Gillian Parkin. "Why
do men always feel they have to *like* women
writers?"

"Is it just that way round? A woman was
telling me yesterday how much she disliked
D. H. Lawrence — "

"Oh well — quite right. The complete
pig."

"Anyway, yes, I could imagine the letters
would arouse a certain interest. Perhaps not
altogether of a literary sort. Of course I was
seeing them as a policeman . . ."

"As a policeman?"

"Yes. I was wondering about the murder-
suicide."

"And was there anything in the letters
about that?"

"Well — of a negative sort," said Charlie,
thoughtfully.

"And what I've been wondering about,"
said Oddie, turning to Vibeke Nordli, "is
your fellow Norwegian."

She nodded vigorously.

"I'm sure you're quite right to. I was curious about him once or twice during the
Weekend, because he never seemed to want
to talk about the Sneddons, and if he couldn't
avoid it he didn't seem to know much about

them. I didn't think much about it then, but after the murder I really did start wondering."

"And?"

"I thought it might be a while before you got around to him and his background, so I rang up this friend in Oslo and asked her to go round and take a look at his bookshop. I rang her again last night, to hear what she'd found out. Well, on the surface it's a perfectly respectable *antikvariat* — which in Norway is usually a combination of antiquarian and ordinary second-hand bookshop. It's in a slightly run-down street, five minutes from the centre. When you look closely at the stock you notice that he has a special interest in loony-Right authors: Hamsun, of course, d'Annunzio, Lawrence, Ayn Rand, Henry Williamson — not, some of them, writers with any obvious appeal in Norway. But what's really interesting is the shop next door."

"Ah."

"It's called Occupation, and it specialises in what it calls souvenirs of the Nazi occupation of Norway. Not the Resistance, note, but the Occupation. In fact it peddles a lot of cheap Nazi mementoes — tin swastikas, iron crosses, posters, that kind of thing — along with a bit of genuine stuff to give it some respectability. My friend said there was no physical connection between the two shops, but the assistant in the souvenir shop had been in the bookshop when she first went in there."

"Very interesting," said Oddie. "But puzzling in a way. The image I have of Norway doesn't suggest there would be a lot of neo-Fascist cranks to provide a market for that kind of thing. Isn't it a time you would rather forget?"

"Twenty years ago the cranks would scarcely have existed. But there's been a big right-wing revival, with a nasty anti-refugee programme. 'Refugee' means anyone non-white — or even non-Scandinavian. I'm afraid the market is there."

"So . . . Here we have Mr Mjølhus in Micklewike, engaged in an underhand deal with Gerald Suzman which I can't go into. Did they clinch it, I wonder? And why didn't he leave as soon as the murder was discovered?"

"Oh, I don't think that would have been a good idea," said Vibeke Nordli, after a moment's thought. "It would have aroused my suspicions immediately. He had told me and others too that he'd be here until Tuesday. In fact that had made me wonder too — combined with his lack of interest in the

Sneddons. After all, there isn't a great deal in Micklewike or in Batley Bridge, unless you're a dedicated walker or a dedicated Sneddon reader. He didn't seem to be either. Why stay on?"

"To conclude the deal with Suzman, I imagine." Mike Oddie turned to Charlie. "It may be we need to take another look at his cottage."

On the drive over to Oxenthorpe Oddie leafed his way though the various reports that had been waiting for him in the Incident Room. The pathologist was inclined towards a late time for Suzman's death: midnight or even one o'clock in the morning. The implement that killed him was probably a heavy iron bar of some kind. There was quite a lot of rust in the wounds. Nothing at the scene of the crime fitted the bill, and the weapon had presumably been taken away after the murder and somehow disposed of. In general Gerald Suzman was a healthy man for his age, and could have expected to live for many years.

"And but for his cleverness he might have," Oddie said, retailing this verdict to Charlie. "Don't you get that feeling — that he had lived all his life on his wits, one clever wheeze after another, and at last he over-reached himself?"

"Oh yes, sure. But the question is: which of the wheezes was the one that proved to be his downfall? If you look at both the current ones we know about, they seem . . . well, they don't seem quite to measure up. The Conference is the biggest thing he'd gone in for so far — the biggest and the most public. But it seems out of all proportion to the current scams that we know about."

"Exactly. The Hamsun letter seems not much more than a nice little sideline: it might have led to further nice little sidelines, but somehow it doesn't seem to amount to anything big, in the context of other things he's been associated with."

"No . . . The Sneddon manuscripts are bigger, of course. There was money in the typescripts if they were accepted as genuine, and — subject to checking with the publishers — we can take it that the new, scholarly editions would bring in a bit of money to him as editor. That was something he was obviously unwilling to share with anyone like Gillian Parkin."

"For obvious reasons."

"True. She might have got on to their bogusness. But he may have been protecting a source of income too. Still, somehow we don't yet seem to be talking big money."

"I suppose we have to ask ourselves if he

had a partner in this, as he obviously had with the Hamsun letter. Did he have a Sneddon expert improvising the dirty bits? If so, why?"

They thought for a bit.

"Nobody springs to mind from the Conference," said Charlie, "apart from Gillian Parkin and Vibeke Nordli. If it was one of them, they're sending up a very good smoke-screen. Rupert Coggenhoe seems to be too obsessed with his own fame to want to contribute to the increase of anyone else's. His participation at the Weekend was self-promotion, not Sneddon promotion . . ."

"Somehow I feel this was a one-man operation," said Oddie.

"So do I. In fact I feel that most of his scams were, though using others to load off the fakes. For anything foreign he would need a native speaker, but otherwise I'd guess he was a sort of literary chameleon: if he saw the opportunity he could write in the manner of anybody he chose. Probably prided himself on it. I suspect he did the Orton fake, and he was in the process of doing the Sneddon fakes. I imagine he rather liked doing 'dirty bits' of any kind."

"I think you're probably right: he'd have rubbed his hands. But where does murder come in?"

"Exactly. I can't see Randolph Sneddon finding out about the forged dirty bits and murdering to protect his relative's reputation. I have a feeling that the whole business of the Sneddon typescripts hasn't come together yet."

When they got to the cottage they pulled off from the road and sat thinking. Then Oddie said:

"I think if we've got time we should take this place apart."

When they got to the cottage gate Charlie said: "Wait." They paused on the little dirt track. The gate to the cottage was wrought-iron, set in a squat little fence with thick iron palings. Some were rotting, and Charlie pointed to a point half-way along the front where one of the palings was missing. They went along silently and examined the gap, particularly where the paling had come away from the crossbars at top and bottom of the fence.

"It looks recent," said Oddie.

"And it looks as if it has been wrenched away by force," Charlie pointed out. "You might expect that sort of vandalism in the city, but not here in the middle of nowhere."

"The doc's report spoke of rust in the wound," said Oddie. "Have we found our weapon?"

"Or *not* found it," said Charlie pessimistically. "It could have been discarded anywhere — in the middle of the moors, miles from here, miles from anywhere. The chances of finding it are virtually nil. But if it was this iron bar that killed him, it does tell us something, doesn't it?"

"It certainly tells us the thing was all but unpremeditated. It tells us that the man — or woman — was desperate, or beyond rational planning. It tells us that he was improvising. Come on, let's go inside."

Inside the cottage they went about their business without further preamble. Charlie went through the books on the unit, flicking through them for letters or papers. Then he crossed the room to another untidy pile on the heavy cupboard over by the window, and here he was lucky. In among a fairly random collection of hardbacks and paperbacks designed for casual reading he found a leather folder, roughly A5 in shape, and inside he found an old, or apparently old, handwritten letter, six pages in length. It began: "Kjære venn!"

"This must be it," he said to Oddie. "The Hamsun letter."

Oddie came over and took it from him in his gloved hand.

"Right!" he said. "We're not going to get

anywhere trying to read it. And I'm not sure our forensic people over here are the best ones to handle it. We'll have to get it physically to Oslo, for tests on the paper, and to get a handwriting expert on to it. As far as we two are concerned there's not much doubt it's a forgery, or that it was Mjølhus who did it. The interesting thing about finding it is the confirmation that it was actually handed over."

"Yes. It could have happened during the Weekend, though," Charlie pointed out. "There was plenty going on all over the shop that I didn't see. On the other hand he could have brought it here. Safer, really, and giving more chance for talk — and maybe negotiation. I wonder if Mjølhus had a car with him."

"Could you get on to Vibeke Nordli and find out? She said he wasn't interested in walking. I've found a stack of things here that seem to be of interest."

So while Oddie was rummaging down in the cupboard at the bottom of the wall unit, Charlie rang the Duke of Cumberland and the Incident Room. As he expected, one of the constables there was able to get hold of Vibeke Nordli, who was still hanging about in the bars exchanging gossip and hoping for developments.

"He didn't have his car with him, but he did hire one," she told him. "He collected it from a car hire firm in Batley Bridge after the Weekend was over. He said he wanted to see a bit of Yorkshire, and so far as I know he did. I didn't see anything of him on Sunday evening, and the only time I saw him on Monday or Tuesday was when he came down here to be interviewed."

"Right. Will you tell this to the constable who fetched you, and ask him to get what details he can from the car firm? By the way, is Lettie still around?"

"Oh yes. Do you want me to fetch her?"

"No — no point in getting her upstairs needlessly. And this is nothing to do with the case. Just ask her, if she does go and see her mother again, if she'd make enquiries about what happened at the farm after the Sneddons' deaths: did the cousin come and take over? Did he try and farm it, or did he sell it immediately — that kind of thing."

"Right, I'll do that."

"And give her my love."

"That's a very unpolicemanly thing to say."

"I'm a very unpolicemanly policeman."

Mike Oddie was now sitting on the floor, his feet stretched out in front of him, sorting through a disorderly mass of papers in the bottom of the cupboard unit.

"He was a pretty unmethodical sort of guy," he said as Charlie finished his phone call and came over to him. "The artistic temperament, no doubt. Electricity bills, bills for servicing the car, letters from Sneddon fans, letters from publishers. Here's one from the people who are going — were going — to do the new edition of the Sneddon novels."

He handed Charlie a letter with the letterhead Bennett and Morley in stylish red lettering at the top.

"There's too many publishers in all this," said Charlie, his forehead crinkling. "Now: the original ones, the ones she went to see, were Carter and Foreman."

"Probably long since gone to the wall," said Oddie. "Or been swallowed up by some big Corporation."

"Right. She did say the big cheese there was interested in books. Probably fatal."

"Almost certainly, They say the men who buy books for W. H. Smith never ever read one, and go entirely on the covers."

"Right. Then the people who led the revival of interest in Susannah were the Untamed Shrew Press."

"Yes. You've got some of their paperbacks."

"Nicely produced. They do a good job. So Bennett and Morley are the people Suzman had got lined up to do the scholarly edition. I wonder if the Untamed Shrew Press people are happy about that."

"Vibeke Nordli said they were a bit snooty about Suzman and the Weekend. Maybe there's a feeling of 'We woz robbed.' "

"Well, they'll be grateful they were never involved when the truth gets out. Let's have a look at this letter."

It was brief and businesslike, and dated December 12th of the previous year.

Dear Mr Suzman,
Thank you for your typescript for the new edition of *The Barren Fields*. I have no doubt you will find that our decision to begin the series with Sneddon's most popular novel, rather than proceed chronologically, will be justified. I anticipate that this first title will arouse a great deal of media interest.

I am glad that all questions of editorial fees, copyright etc. have now been sorted out, and I can set a firm publishing date for October. I will be sending you art-work for the cover in the course of the next month or so.

Yes, I have noted that a Yorkshire

firm is to reissue the Joshua Sneddon novels. No, as you apparently realize, a new scholarly edition of them would be of no interest to us.

With best wishes,
Deborah Vigne

"Not very exciting," commented Charlie.

"As opposed to this," said Mike Oddie, handing him a piece of typing paper. "Modern paper, you note. But it's dummy runs for some of the hot passages."

"Oh my!" said Charlie appreciatively. " 'Heaving breasts . . . screams of pleasure . . . felt his hardness . . .' Wasn't he having a good time!"

"I think it would be a kindness to ring this Deborah Vigne and tell her to put the brakes on her new edition. It will be money down the drain for them. How shall we put it? 'Serious doubts have arisen about the authenticity of Gerald Suzman's new texts.' Sounds good. Look — I've collected everything that might be of interest. Let's get back to Batley Bridge."

"Do you think it's worth having another word with Mrs Tuckett while we're here?" Charlie asked. "These country people don't come forward with information very readily, and it may be some other member of her family saw something that night."

But when she answered the door Mrs Tuckett shook her head to their questions.

"Oh no. I've asked my daughter, naturally. I'm afraid we've talked about little else since you were last here. She was fast asleep like me that night."

"Suzman was a bit of a night bird, wasn't he?" Oddie asked.

"Oh yes. If I did get up in the night, there'd often be lights on there. 'Who needs sleep?' he used to say. 'A most unproductive activity.' He used to talk like that — quite a character, was Mr Suzman. I've got to say I'll miss him. I had reason to be grateful to him. The money he paid me to keep an eye on the place and clean it came in useful, and so did the little bit he paid for the garage when he was up here. It's not easy making ends meet these days."

"You're a widow?"

"These ten years. My daughter's working now, which helps, and there's a bit of money comes in from the bed and breakfast people, but with the cost of living going up the whole time it's still a bit of a struggle."

"Did you have a bed and breakfast guest the night of the Suzman murder?" Charlie asked.

"Oh yes. He was a walker. I have to get

up early every morning, because my daughter's job is in Bradford, and she has to get the bus, but that morning I remember I was extra early because he wanted to be off and away. That's why I was early over to the cottage with the parcel."

"Do you remember your guest's name? It's just possible he saw something."

"I don't, I'm afraid. It wasn't one of my regulars. Anyway he couldn't have seen anything because the guest bedroom's at the front, and the toilet window's frosted."

"Another avenue closed," commented Charlie.

"I wouldn't have your job for the world, for all it's well-paid," said Mrs Tuckett sympathetically. "If you want my opinion, you'll find there's a woman there somewhere. I knew the minute I clapped eyes on him that Mr Suzman was one for the ladies."

"Oh, there's a woman there somewhere," said Charlie, as they trudged back to their car. "Her name's Susannah Sneddon."

"And everyone's fighting over her," agreed Mike. "It's a bit like a B-grade Western, isn't it?"

"With the Dolores del Rio figure sixty years dead," agreed Charlie. "Fair makes you shiver!" he added cheerfully.

Chapter 18

Glimmerings

As he went about a mountain of humdrum tasks in and around the Duke of Cumberland, Charlie registered with pleasure that Felicity Coggenhoe had arrived from Leeds. She mingled with the others marking time at the place without any problem: away from her parents she was relaxed and uncomplicated. There was in any case a sort of fellowship of ghouls that seemed to break down barriers. The landlord smiled on them, and on Charlie and Mike Oddie, with a complacency that said that, as far as he was concerned, the district could have a murder a week and he wouldn't complain.

"Lettie's up at the Home seeing her mother," Felicity told him, during a snatched exchange in the inn's foyer. "I gather there was something you wanted to know."

"Yes. Just personal interest. Nothing to

289

do with the case. What are you doing afterwards?"

"Most of them feel they need a change from this place. The bar-food menu is pretty monotonous. We thought we might go along to the Chinese restaurant."

"Good idea. I agree with Suzman that a super-hygienic restaurant is a contradiction in terms. Are all of you going?"

"Gillian's waiting for her boyfriend to turn up from his walking tour. If he does they'll be with us. If not it's just Lettie, Vibeke and me."

"I might try to join you, but don't expect me."

"All right. I'll just hope."

"Nice! I can't talk about the case, of course."

"Of course not. I can't say I'll mind. So far we don't seem to have talked about anything else."

About seven o'clock Charlie, from the upstairs window of the Incident Room, saw three of them setting out, Lettie hobbling gamely. Twenty minutes later he was able to wind up his work and was given the rest of the day off. Mike Oddie said he thought he might join them, but he was niggled by the thought there was something else to do that he'd forgotten. "If it comes to me I'll join you later," he said.

At the Mah Fung the three women had commandeered a large table, on the grounds that their party might be expanding. The place was less than half full, probably because much of their likely clientele was hovering around the Duke of Cumberland. Charlie kissed Lettie, then sank into the chair opposite beside Felicity, where the menu was waiting for him. He looked around him: red flock wallpaper and cheap lampshades with a faint look of Chinese lanterns. It was like every small-town Chinese restaurant he had ever been in.

"The secret is the cooking," said Vibeke Nordli.

"And the bugs in the kitchen," added Charlie. He scanned the menu, which was more selective, less of an omnium gatherum, than most such establishments boasted.

"Pork and beansprouts, prawns and cashews, and fried rice," he told the blandly hovering waiter. "I feel like I haven't eaten since Sunday."

"How do you exist when you're on an important case?" asked Vibeke Nordli. "Norwegians always have to have their regular meals."

"Regular meal people shouldn't become policemen," Charlie said grandly.

"Perhaps it's a good thing there's not much crime in Norway, then."

"Don't you believe it! It sounds to me as though you've got it, but nobody finds out about it. Too busy eating their regular meals." He turned to Lettie. "And how are you, dear lady, as Mr Suzman would have said? How did you get on at Casa Geriatrica?"

"Don't laugh at the old, Dexter," Lettie reproved him. "I'm on the brink myself. And whatever else you can say about my mother, if she was geriatric she wouldn't be much use to you, would she? Well, of course she was as grouchy as usual about my wanting to ask her about the Sneddons. She thinks I ought only to be interested in *her* — but what in hell's name is there to talk about? The weather? What she had for dinner? What was on the goddamn box last night? Actually she refuses to watch the box — says it's sinful, which sounds to me like the right deed for the wrong reason, but that's typical of my mother."

"But you eventually got her round to it, did you?"

"Don't rush me, Dexter. I may be a New Yorker but I like to go at my own pace. Well, we talked about when I was coming back to Britain to make a home for her, and I said when the dollar picked up. That should be safe enough. Then we somehow got round to the Methodist Chapel in the old days — a real fun topic that, I can tell you! Eventually I got it round to funerals, and the Sneddon funeral in particular, and that set her off. Hardly anybody went, but everyone knew about it and watched from darkened rooms."

"Why did hardly anybody go? Because they weren't popular?"

"Not so much that, because funerals were an event in village life, and you didn't have to be popular to draw a good crowd. No, it was because of the shame: suicides were a shame and an embarrassment, and a murder-suicide — well, people didn't want to have anything to do with it."

"A bit primitive."

"We were."

"So who went?"

"Oh, the schoolmaster, the doctor, and suchlike: the respectable people, the un-superstitious ones. After all, Susannah was *known*, a definite name, and from the village. They felt that respect should be paid. And then there was the cousin — George Sneddon from Abbotsford. His wife too, though she was pregnant. That would be with the father of Heathcliff, I would think. That was about it, really."

"Was it a 'good' funeral?"

"Middling, my mother says. Not a 'no expense spared' job, but better than the village had expected, given that Cousin George had the reputation of a skinflint."

"Had George Sneddon taken over at High Maddox by then?"

"Oh yes. Came over and installed himself there soon as the bodies were taken away almost. Said the farm needed all his time to get it round, after Joshua had all but ruined it. And to give him his due, Mother says that he did get it round, to the degree that he could sell it. That was all he was interested in doing. As soon as it was in better shape he put it on the market and took the best offer. And a bit later he sold his own farm and moved South. Said the North was finished. A lot thought that in those days. I'm not sure I didn't myself."

"Any idea what he did down there?"

"Set up in his own business somewhere in Essex, so they said in the village. Builder and decorator. Always a very handy person, Cousin George."

"Do you have any recollection of him, personal recollection?" asked Vibeke Nordli.

"Precious little," replied Lettie, considering. "He was never much around the village, I think, and he wasn't one to socialise. If he wasn't at the farm he was at Abbotsford. But he did sometimes come to the Methodist Chapel, so I saw him there. Tight, mean little mouth and eyes."

"Do you remember the funeral?"

"Yes, I do. That whole week, from the deaths to the funeral. My brother and I watched the coffins coming down the hill from the farm, then turning right towards the churchyard. They all walked in procession — no cars. They weren't buried in the Methodist plot, which must have been a big relief to all us Methodies, but in the parish churchyard, and the service was in the parish church. You were assumed to be Church of England in those days if you never showed signs of having a religion."

"Makes sense," said Charlie. "You say the week after their deaths. There wasn't any great delay before the bodies were released, then?"

"Oh no. The village constable was Tom Harker — big, stupid chap, whose idea of law-enforcement was spanking kids who'd been caught stealing apples. But they sent someone up from Batley Bridge, or maybe from Halifax, and they were perfectly clear about what had happened. So the funeral went ahead quite quickly, and George Sneddon took over at the farm."

"And he wasn't liked in the village either, I suppose?" Charlie asked.

"Not greatly, Dexter, from what I remember. They thought he was getting above himself — they always hated that in Micklewike, and they had a great variety of words for people who did. Oddly enough, they didn't resent his inheriting the farm — that was natural, according to their way of thinking. But they did resent his getting money from the books. He must have got the advance for *The Black Byre* — the one that was just finished when she was killed — as well as anything still coming in from the earlier ones. My mother said this afternoon: 'He never wrote them books. He'd no right to take money for them.' That must have been what people said at the time: my mother nurses every little grudge and resentment she's ever known, even if they are not hers. But it was a very illogical line to take. After all, if he hadn't had the money, who would have had it? And if you can inherit a farm, why not royalties? But she just shook her head grimly when I said that."

"But I think a lot of people may feel like that," said Felicity. "People get a good feeling out of Bernard Shaw's royalties going to the British Museum. You don't get such a good feeling out of royalties going to the not particularly talented children of great writers."

"And an awful lot of great writers seem to have had untalented children," said Lettie. "But it *is* illogical."

"She didn't mean it personally about children of great writers," said Charlie, turning to Felicity with a grin.

"I'm not the child of a great writer," said Felicity. "Nor anything remotely approaching one."

"There was something you said," Charlie took up, with a frown on his face, "something you said when we talked yesterday in Leeds. Was it about the *re*-establishment of a copyright? Surely that isn't possible, is it? Not if an author has been dead for fifty years?"

"Oh, but it is, nowadays. Something to do with a recent Copyright Act. I know it's happened in the case of D. H. Lawrence. And that's pretty funny in itself . . ."

"Why?" asked Lettie.

"Because when Frieda Lawrence died the people who inherited the rights and the royalties were the children she had left behind when she ran off with Lawrence. Her children by Ernest Weekley, who was a professor of English at Nottingham. That's a pretty odd way for them to end up, though

I suppose you could say there's a sort of poetic justice."

"But this about re-establishing copyright," insisted Charlie, forking in food that was, indeed, glorious.

"Well, as I say, it's recent, and I don't know all that much about it. What happened in the case of Lawrence was that a new edition of the books came out — a scholarly edition from the manuscripts, with a lot of stuff the original publisher had censored. This edition superseded the old ones, and you couldn't reprint or even quote from them, or the new ones, without permission. So in essence the copyright was re-established."

"And the heirs — or the heirs of the heirs of the heirs, or whatever — go on enjoying royalties for another fifty years?"

"Something like that. I'm no expert, as I say, but I did look into the Lawrence situation when I was thinking of doing him for my thesis subject. The main thing is that editorial work is done, and new material added. Then copyright can legally be re-established. I think something of the same sort is happening with James Joyce and Scott Fitzgerald."

"Oh my!" said Charlie, but he said it to himself.

They were interrupted by an incursion — Gillian Parkin, arm in arm with Gregory Waite, looking tanned and fit from his walking holiday, both of them obviously overjoyed at being in each other's company again. Trailing in their wake was Mike Oddie.

Charlie took advantage of all the introductions and the arrangement of chairs and places to slip aside with his boss.

"Did you remember what you'd forgotten to do?" he asked.

"No — it's eluded me. I thought I needed a bite — "

"It wasn't to ring that woman at Bennett and Morley's, the publishers, was it?"

"Damn!" said Oddie violently. "Yes, it was. I'll go back and do it now."

"No, I'll go. You must be hungry."

"No, you stay here. They're all young people, apart from your elderly girlfriend. They'll be constrained by me, but they will probably talk more freely with you. I should have done it before, because they could stand to lose a lot of money with that edition. I don't suppose it will take long. Vigne's not a particularly common name."

"Well, when you get on to her, ask about copyright."

"Copyright?"

"In particular the re-establishment of copyright."

"I didn't know you could. Do you think it's relevant?"

"I do. Please Mike, make a point of it. You know, there's something that bothered me quite early on in this case, and I've just remembered what it was."

"What was it?"

"Let's just say it's musical. Think on't, as you say in Yorkshire."

"I do hate a cockney smartarse," said Oddie, hurrying away.

At the table the newcomers were settling in and orders were being taken. Charlie let them take away his conspicuously cleared plates, and ordered the inevitable lychees and another glass of wine. Gregory Waite was reading the menu as if it were the *News of the World*, and ordering dishes on a gargantuan scale.

"I've been eating as and when I could," he explained to excuse himself. "And I've always said that the old canard about being hungry again soon after a Chinese meal doesn't apply if only you eat enough."

"We've been doing nothing but sitting around in bars nibbling and drinking," said Gillian. "I'll just have little bits of whatever you're eating. By now murder has dulled the appetite."

"Oh yes, murder," said Gregory, with a smile of relish. "What a thing to miss! There's me been tramping all over the moors thinking wholesome thoughts, and you've been living in the middle of a glorious sensation. I wish now I'd stayed for the Weekend. How was he murdered?"

"Bludgeoned," said Gillian, glancing at Charlie but leaving him out of it. "Somehow it doesn't seem an appropriate way for him to go."

"Stiletto would have been better," agreed Lettie. "Or some subtle poison. He was a subtle guy."

"I never saw him, remember," said Gregory. "I went off on the first morning of the Conference."

"Well," said Felicity, "he was a rather pleased-with-himself, soft-living sort of a man — plump, devious, not-to-be-pinned-down."

"Sybaritic," said Gillian. "And up to something."

"Did you realize that at the time?"

"No," she said ruefully. "I was fooled because I wanted to be fooled."

"And what was he up to?"

"Forgery," said Vibeke Nordli bitterly. "Among other things, probably."

"And someone battered him to death, did you say, Gillian? How exactly? What were the circumstances?"

They all looked at Charlie.

"Someone seems to have called on him late at night, and when he answered the door he was battered to death in the little hallway."

Gregory's brow furrowed. He turned to Gillian.

"But we looked through the windows of the farm on Friday evening. It's one big room. There isn't a hallway."

Gillian shook her head.

"I didn't say he was murdered at the farm. It was in his own cottage."

"Sorry. Stupid of me. I knew he owned it, and I assumed he had quarters there."

"Oh no," said Charlie. "When he was up here he lived in his cottage in Oxenthorpe."

"Oxenthorpe?"

It was said a mite too loudly, and Charlie could have sworn that something — a shadow, a memory — passed over Gregory's face.

"Yes, a cottage just before you get to the village, on the road from Batley Bridge."

"Oh."

"Do you know Oxenthorpe?"

"I stayed there overnight," said Waite, choosing his words with care. "I only camp

302

out alternate nights."

"It wasn't Sunday night, was it?"

"No, it wasn't Sunday. Tuesday, I think."

Charlie held his peace. He ate his lychees, which he thought a remarkably uninteresting fruit, and halfway through his second glass of wine, while the conversation was ranging from conjecture to misunderstanding, he slipped out of his seat and went to the lavatory. It was a matter of seconds before he heard the door open and someone was standing beside him.

"Can we talk?"

"Yes. When?"

"It would be difficult now. Too obvious."

"Tomorrow morning early?"

"Yes. I'm not a breakfast person. I could tell Gillian I have to get something from the Chemist's. I'm asthmatic."

"You could come along to my b. and b. place. Forty Haworth Road. I'll get Oddie along."

"Right . . . Thanks."

Charlie ruminated as he zipped his fly that he had once done business with a snout in a public urinal while he was with the Metropolitan Police. It wasn't something he would have expected to happen in rural Yorkshire.

Chapter 19

Unravelling

Mrs Ludlum was over the moon at the prospect of two extra men for breakfast.

"One will just have toast and tea," Charlie explained. "I should think the other would appreciate the whole caboodle."

"No problem," said Mrs Ludlum. "Though it might mean slightly short commons for you."

"Oh, *please*," said Charlie, but silently. Then aloud: "If you could get everything on the table, then disappear. Sorry to put it like that. This may be important and we can't do with interruptions. When the case is over I'll nip across and tell you everything that went on. But till then . . ."

She nodded, hardly disguising her reluctance. She never actually listened outside doors, but she did sometimes find, with her hands full, that it was a long time before she could find a way to turn the handle. But next morning she was as good as her word. When the three men were assembled in the front room she brought cereals, tea, toast and two laden plates and then, with a last appraising look at the newcomers, she disappeared back to the kitchen with all the enthusiasm of Macbeth going off to murder Duncan.

"You saw it in my face, didn't you?" Gregory Waite said to Charlie.

"Yes, I did. And I heard it in your voice."

Gregory toyed with a butter-knife and an unwanted slice of toast.

"I'd make an awful criminal . . . But I think I'll be all right as a witness, if it should come to that . . . I'm hoping that maybe he'll confess, whoever he is. Or that we can somehow arrange any evidence I have to give so that — "

"So that the sleeping arrangements that night at your b. and b. don't have to come out?"

Gregory gave a lop-sided smile.

"Yes."

"I don't see why they should. I take it you were sleeping in one of the back bedrooms?"

Gregory sighed.

"Yes . . . Gillian's a strong-minded girl,

and I want to marry her. She's very much the monogamous type — says it's the only sensible thing to be these days, but really it's the old puritanism in a new guise. I'm afraid I'm just not the faithful type."

"We're policemen, not father confessors," Oddie pointed out.

"OK, OK, I'm just talking to myself. It's my problem."

"So you were in fact in Mrs Tuckett's daughter's bedroom," Charlie pursued.

"Yes. Well, in both hers and mine, actually. Mrs Tuckett went up to bed around ten. Then things sort of . . . developed, with both of us giving the usual signals, and by the time we went up the stairs the mother was snoring and somehow it was inevitable."

"I know how it is."

"I knew I'd have to be back in my room by morning. She'd said she'd bring me an early-morning cup of tea. I woke up around one . . ." He thought back, frowning. "I don't know whether something woke me up. I think that must have been it, because as I was creeping out I automatically pulled the curtain aside to look out."

"Over to the cottage?"

"Yes. The girl had told me that a literary gentleman lived there. That's why I suddenly connected up last night. There'd been a light on there when we went to bed, and it was still on. And there was this figure at the door. I suppose it may have been his knocking that woke me . . ."

He stopped, remembering.

"What's wrong?"

"He was holding something in his hand, but . . . behind his leg, hidden. I think I should have known then. Not that I could have done anything . . . Carol Tuckett was fast asleep — just like her mother, that one. She'd got what she'd been after (well, so had I, I have to admit), and she was out to the world. I stood there watching. I must have been uneasy . . . After a few minutes the door was opened, they swapped a few words, and then the visitor was ushered inside."

"Could you see either of them?"

"No. The visitor had his back to me, of course. He was tall, well set-up, and he masked the one who opened the door. I stood there . . . There *must* have been something nagging away inside me . . . Then after a minute or two he came out, shut the door, and began striding through the garden, then down the lane to the road. He was still carrying something — not hiding it now, but carrying it carefully. I tiptoed out of the room, along the landing and into my own bedroom. I went to the window, and he was getting into his car — a little sporty job, two-seater. He was putting whatever he was carrying against the passenger seat — gingerly I thought. Then he started up and sped off."

"Did you watch him? Did he ever stop?"

"For a minute or two. No, he didn't. But you'd go a fair way before you'd throw away a weapon, wouldn't you? If that's what it was."

"Oh, that's what it was. Did you ever see his face?"

"For a moment, when he came out of the cottage. Not well, because the light was behind him in the cottage, not over him."

"Could you identify him?"

"I don't know . . . I'd rather not have to, but possibly . . . What I got was hardly more than an impression."

"And what was the impression?" Oddie asked.

"That he was very, very handsome."

"To tell you the truth, I'm not quite sure why you are here," said Randolph Sneddon. "I told you all I know on Tuesday. Naturally I've thought — racked my brains — to try to come up with anything else, anything I've forgotten, but nothing's surfaced. I'd have rung you if it had."

He was walking up and down in his Notting Hill flat, but this time the nervous energy that Mike and Charlie had noticed before had a tenseness to it that suggested he sensed danger. There was a feeling that desperation was just around the corner, and Charlie wondered what it would take to make him crack.

"Well, let's get back to that visit you made to the cottage on Sunday evening, sir," said Oddie. "Just for a friendly chat about the Committee and suchlike."

"That's right."

"He had music on the CD player, I believe?"

"Did he? Now you come to mention it, yes, he did. Don't ask me what — I've no ear for classical music. Some romantic symphony or other, I'd guess."

"Odd that," said Charlie, "to keep loud music playing while you're having a chat with a guest. You might imagine some teenage yob doing that, but not a man who rather pushed his artistic sensibilities at you, as Suzman did."

"I bow to your knowledge of the artistic temperament, but that's what happened. Maybe he wasn't so cultivated as he gave out. Don't ask me — I hardly knew the man."

"The only reason I can think of to keep loud music playing during a private conversation," said Oddie, "is that there was a likelihood of its becoming a row. And when it comes down to it, it does seem a bit incredible that you would go by car all the way over to Oxenthorpe to tell him you were unlikely to be a very active Committee member. Three lines on a postcard or a quick phone call could have told him that."

"I had time to waste."

"Why? Why not drive home that evening?"

"I like night driving. It's the only time I can let rip in the Porsche."

"I must say I regard that meeting at around seven as a falling-out of partners. Because that's what you were, isn't it?"

Randolph Sneddon shook his head with the guardsmanlike decisiveness that now seemed to Charlie such a sham.

"Certainly not. The only sense in which we were partners was that we were both Committee members of — "

"I'm not talking about the Sneddon Fellowship. I'm talking about the new edition of Susannah Sneddon's novels, copyrighted in your name. Bringing you royalties for the next fifty years."

He brushed aside the suggestion with his large, capable hand.

"Some kind of legal technicality, Suzman said. Naturally it's not the kind of thing I have any experience in."

"That's not the impression I got when I talked to Deborah Vigne, at Bennett and Morley's. She said there were long and detailed negotiations. I rather think that when we start digging with the lawyers we shall find an agreement between you — an agreement specifying the division of the spoils."

The hand fluttered, less decisively.

"No . . . Well, now you mention it, I do seem to remember — "

"Because what we're talking about is royalties for probably the rest of your life on twelve books — and with Susannah Sneddon's star in the ascendent that means a very considerable sum of money. Particularly with Suzman knowing all the tricks to make sure her star remains in the ascendent."

"I couldn't see — can't see — any harm in re-establishing the family's rights in the books."

"But already your connection with Suzman is a lot closer than you've been willing to tell us about so far, isn't it? How did you divide the expected loot? Fifty-fifty? Or did he want more, as the man who was cobbling together the fake manuscripts?"

"Fake manuscripts? I had no idea — "

He was crumbling rapidly, and the two policemen decided to go in for the kill. Charlie started off.

"All this is a bit irrelevant, really," he said, leaning forward. "In view of what we know about your second visit to Moor View Cottage on Sunday night . . ."

"Second visit? There was no second visit."

"Oh, but there was!" said Charlie, leaning back in his chair. "Around one o'clock. You left your Porsche by the road and went up to the cottage. You'd seen the rotting palings in the fence earlier, and you went and wrenched one out."

"That may count in your favour at the trial," put in Oddie, as the two switched into a sort of duet. "You didn't go prepared with a weapon."

"Then you went and banged on the door."

"Suzman was still up — he needed very little sleep. You stood there, with the heavy iron bar behind your leg. And when he let you in you attacked him in the little hallway with it, and left him for dead. And that was when you made your mistake."

"Because if you'd switched the lights off,

our witness wouldn't have seen you as you came out."

"Though we'd still have your car to go on."

"As it was he saw you clearly. We can arrange an identity parade, and we're quite confident he will pick you out."

"He saw you against the light, still carrying the iron bar. And he saw you put it into your car. We'll be taking the Porsche into custody, sir. Forensic can do wonders these days. Even if we never find the murder weapon they can compare traces with other bars from that fence. We've got a motive, we've got a witness, and we'll have conclusive forensic evidence. I think when you get your lawyer he'll tell you to plead manslaughter."

It was the mention of Forensic that seemed to do the damage. In Oddie's view people had the most credulous notions — perhaps fed by articles in the popular press — about what the new techniques in forensic science can do. It had become a sort of modern superstition. Randolph Sneddon hardly tried any longer to hide how shaken he was. His hand was far from steady as he went to the bar, poured himself the stiffest whisky yet, and splashed it with soda. He walked around the room, gulped at his drink, then sat down facing them.

"How did I get into this mess?" he asked, choking.

"Money?" suggested Oddie.

"Yes, money . . . Gambling has always been my passion. People assume it's women, because I'm a fairly good-looking guy. But all the big mistakes I make are about money. When things started cracking up in the City I tried to recoup some of my losses by gambling. The mug's answer. But I've always loved the tables — and a couple of years ago I started going to casinos practically every night. With the predictable result. That's where I met Suzman."

"He was a gambler too?"

"An occasional one. For him it added spice to a night out. Sensible man. We met at the Cockatoo, in Mayfair. Very exclusive, very expensive if you lose. We got talking in the bar, and when he told me he was a bookseller and generally somebody in the literary world I let fall that I was related to Susannah Sneddon. It was just a way of keeping the conversation going, really. I felt a bit out of my depth."

"Did he show interest at once?"

"Not obviously. But he gave me his card, and got mine in return. Then we went back in, and he watched me losing. I suppose he

314

investigated the position with regard to the Sneddon copyright, and the manuscripts. Her original publishers, Carter and Foreman, went under just after the war. Most of their archives and stock had been destroyed in the Blitz anyway. If anyone asked Suzman he said he retrieved the typescripts from the warehouse of the publishers who took over the name of Carter and Foreman in 1948, but it wasn't true. Of course he was concocting them himself."

"And you came to an agreement with him?"

There was a pause, and then the voice seemed to come from a great ravine.

"Yes. That was the moment, wasn't it? The moment when I stepped into it, irretrievably. Of course we had the alternative scenario well-documented, if anyone should enquire. If you'd wanted to see Suzman's original letter enquiring if I was Susannah Sneddon's relative I could have shown it to you. But in fact we cooked it up between us, and had an agreement signed and sealed: the manuscripts remained his property, but the copyright was to be renewed, and we'd go halves on the royalties from the books . . . It seemed a harmless enough scheme."

"But you knew the typescripts were faked?"

"Why do you think I panicked when — "

"When the scheme blew up in your faces? Or seemed likely to. Yes, of course. But tell me more about this Sneddon Fellowship business."

"It was Suzman's wheeze, of course, to ensure that interest grew and grew. What had he got to lose? He acquired the farm at a rock-bottom price. He was around the area, sniffing out what anybody remembered about the Sneddons and their writing habits, and he saw it was up for sale. He thought it would make an ideal centre — and if need be, when farming land was profitable again, it could be sold. So the Sneddon Fellowship could be centred in Micklewike — ideal. I went along with the idea. He told me there were literary societies for just about every author these days — Arthur Ransome, Angela Thirkell, people I'd never even heard of. So he bought up a lot of junk furniture from shops in Yorkshire and turned it into a sort of museum. I thought it was all pretty clever, frankly. He only claimed one or two things as actually theirs."

"In fact nothing was?" Charlie asked.

"Nothing that I know of. It was all dispersed sixty years ago. Who would keep and cherish a typewriter because Joshua Sneddon had written his novels on it? No, it was all vaguely of the period, that's all."

"But you had no doubts about getting involved with this Weekend," Charlie asked.

"Not really, at the time. A bit nervous about hobnobbing with all those culture vultures. I think I said something like that to you on that first night . . . If I'd known who you were — *what* you were — I'd sure as hell have been nervous . . . But I thought I could play my part all right, because it *wasn't* a part. I was the only living relative of the Sneddons, and I didn't know a great deal about their novels. And it all went well for a bit. There were a lot of elderly enthusiasts, not too high-powered, and I put on the charm for them. It wasn't difficult, and from all I could see Suzman was carrying it off very well."

"When did things start going off the rails?"

"Well, I suppose I started getting worried at the wine and cheese party. That girl going on about the manuscripts — two girls, in fact. And I thought: these people *know* something about Susannah Sneddon. They want to see the manuscripts, and when they do they're going to spot that they're fakes."

"I doubt they would have," Charlie interjected. "They wanted to believe. It's like miracles: if you want to believe *enough*, you do."

"Maybe. But they got me nervous. They showed me that it wasn't as *easy* as I'd thought, not as foolproof. And then people were talking about this couple with letters from Susannah. And perhaps because I was already nervous, *that* got me jumpy too: I hadn't expected that, and neither had Suzman. They were a bolt from the blue for him too. He was *very* keen to get his hands on them, because he feared what I feared: there'd be something in them that showed that the typescripts were fakes."

"There was," said Charlie.

"What was it?"

"There were only ever hand-written manuscripts. That's what the publisher sent to the printers."

Randolph Sneddon's mouth dropped with disbelief.

"My God! In the twentieth century! I can't believe it. That wasn't what I was afraid of at all. I thought maybe she might have said something in the letters about the publishers always accepting what she wrote, never asking for cuts, never trying to censor — that kind of thing. Because that would have exposed the typescripts and knocked the new edition on the head straight away. And then there was that American woman . . ."

"Lettie Farraday," said Oddie. "She had

the best knowledge of the Sneddons of anyone there."

"That's right. She wasn't particularly a
danger that I could see, but she set me thinking: if there was a hand-written manuscript
and it turned up — any one, for any of the
novels — that would expose the typescripts
even more definitely than any letter could.
No hired typist was going to hot up someone
else's novel. Suddenly it all began to seem
dicey, dangerous. Because I had even more
to lose than Suzman: the Stock Exchange
protects its own where it can, but its writ
doesn't extend to straight criminal matters
outside the markets. If I'd been tried, even
if the charge was relatively minor, I'd have
been finished, washed up."

"So what did you do?"

He cradled his glass in his strong hands.

"I suppose I panicked. After the Sunday
meeting I talked to Suzman — apparently
about dates for Committee meetings, but I
whispered to him that he had to get his
hands on those letters. He took that ghastly
looking couple off to lunch and sweet-talked
them as only he knew how, but it was still
no go. 'No luck as yet, dear boy,' he said
airily to me after the lecture. By then I was
trying to be seen talking to him as little as
possible. I made small-talk with the hoi-

polloi, and one of the things that kept coming up was the letters. 'Wasn't it wonderful that there were some, and to an intimate friend? We'd learn so much about their home life, and the inspiration for the books.' It was driving me out of my mind! So when everything was over I tanked up in the Duke of Cumberland and drove over to Suzman's cottage."

"What was his attitude?"

"Still airy."

"He didn't see the dangers?"

"He said if everything went wrong he could brazen it out. He'd done it often enough in the past."

"That was true enough."

"But it was different this time. He'd told me about some of his clever wheezes, and then he'd made sure to keep his distance from the money transaction. This time he was in the centre of the frame. I said this, and he just waved it aside. I said 'You've got to keep me out of it entirely,' and he said 'You're in it, dear boy. There is no risk-free way of making lots of money.' "

"Well, *he* found that out soon enough," commented Charlie.

Randolph Sneddon looked ahead, seeming not to hear.

"Things started to get heated then, and

he turned the music up loud. I told him he had to get hold of those letters at once. He thought about that, and said it was just possible the Potter-Hodges were staying in the Batley Bridge area and wouldn't be home. He hadn't bothered to ask — he was too airy by half. He said he'd go over to Ilkley and investigate after dark."

"He wasn't above a spot of burglary, then?" Oddie asked.

"Oh no. And I got the impression he'd have known how to go about it. I'd have liked something done about that old American bag, but it just wasn't on."

"Somebody 'doing something' about her was just what I feared," said Charlie. "Why wasn't it on?"

"Once what she said about Susannah not typing was out, it was out. People would remember, even if she was out of the way. Added to which, we couldn't have two incidents connecting back to the Fellowship Weekend in one night. And Suzman wasn't a murderer."

"Whereas you, you found, were."

"It was manslaughter! Anyway, the neighbour came in at that point and broke things up. I think I carried things off well enough with her. But I was out of my mind. I went back to Batley Bridge and had a bit more in the bar. Then I went to my room and had a whisky or three there. About half past eleven I thought he might be back and I rang him. 'Nothing doing, dear boy. They were home, and so was their damned great dog. I saw him in the window — Rottweiler or some such thing. But don't *worry*, dear boy. Something will turn up.' I screamed an obscenity at him and hung up. By now I knew I had to do something about him."

"Murder was already on your mind, was it?"

"*No!* . . . But I knew that there was very little to connect me with him, apart from my gracing the Weekend as the last representative of the Sneddon family. With him out of the way . . . I threw things into a case, got in the car and drove off . . . not knowing what I was going to do, I swear."

Oddie and Charlie both took that with a pinch of salt.

"But by the time you got to the cottage you knew?"

"No! . . . Well, I suppose it was an option. I had a heavy spanner in the car. But I thought how messy it would be, and slow, and I'd noticed that rusty fence, with the thick, heavy palings. I suppose by the time I'd wrenched one of those out I'd decided. When he opened the door and said 'Dear boy, lovely to see you, of course, but you're making much too much of this' I just . . . knocked him down. He was half turned away, but he saw it coming. I went on hitting until I knew he was dead, then I came away. God, what a fool I was, not turning off the lights. Somehow I didn't want to go right into the cottage. I just wanted to get away . . . There's not much more to say, is there?"

"Not much," said Oddie. "Randolph Sneddon, I am charging you with the murder of Gerald Suzman . . ."

Later that night, in the dining room of the hotel they had treated themselves to at the West Yorkshire Police Authority's expense, Charlie paused, his knife about to cut into a thick steak, and said:

"I'm not happy about the murder-suicide, you know."

"I know," sighed Oddie. "You're going to look into it. Ah well — I suppose it's a few degrees more current than the Princes in the Tower."

"Of course I'm not saying that murder goes in families — "

"I should hope not. 'Bad blood' and all that sort of thing went out with Agatha Christie."

"All right. But you do get families with

a nasty streak in them."

"Maybe," said Oddie, remembering an earlier case.

"That's all I'm saying."

"But kids more often react against their parents, rather than following them."

"Not in the case of Vidkun Mjølhus," Charlie pointed out. They had had a nice little wad of information on that gentleman from the Oslo police the day before. "He was born in Brazil after his parents got out of Norway in 1945, in the nick of time, but he swallowed their line after the war hook, line and sinker. Anyway, I'm talking about grandfather and grandson. They say things often skip a generation."

"Spare me the pop genetics. Tell me what you have to go on."

"I read those letters. I never once got the feeling that Joshua was jealous of Susannah's greater success. Or even particularly bitter about his own lack of it. He accepted it, fatalistically. And although he didn't greatly like her books he always defended them when they were attacked. I got the feeling of a rather good man — wounded by his war experiences, sometimes rather desperate, melancholic. But I didn't get any sense of jealousy at all."

"Maybe Susannah was such an egotist

she didn't register it."

"They were alone together every evening of their lives. She was an egotist, but she'd have registered it. I think she'd even have enjoyed telling her friend about it, if it had existed. I don't think she was a particularly pleasant person."

"The talk in the village was that he was jealous."

"It would be, wouldn't it? Granted that situation, that's just what the village people were bound to say. Particularly if there was some prompting."

"From Cousin George?"

"Exactly. From the grandfather of our man. He knew them as well as anybody. If he started putting it around locally that Joshua was jealous of his sister's success it would be accepted, and embroidered on."

"So when the deaths came, they would be accepted as a murder, followed by a suicide?"

"Of course. But think how easily there could have been a different interpretation. He shoots Joshua through the head in the spinney ('Just over for a spot of shooting, Cousin Josh'). He was shot through the head, you notice. Most suicides do it through the mouth, but that would have been an impossible murder. Anyway, in a rural area no one would think twice about a shot. Then he goes and has a cousinly chat with Susannah, and in the course of it he takes the axe from the woodpile by the fire and kills her. Scrawls a few words in something approximating Joshua's writing, and Bingo! I get the impression that the investigation was pretty perfunctory. Why have the handwriting checked when it was obvious what had happened? Even that nasty little touch of the cigarette stubbed out on her corpse was witness to the hatred and jealousy everyone took for granted by then. And there was nobody else who had cause to feel that about Susannah."

"Hmmm. The motive at least is obvious. But is it strong enough?"

"Good old *cui bono?* Not just the farm, remember. Susannah was getting one hundred-fifty pound advances on her later books, and there was one just finished. The books earned their advances and more. There'd be money coming in for a few years after her death, and probably money in the bank too, because I have the impression she spent next to nothing, apart from small subsidies to the farm. So in the grinding poverty of that region at that time, there was property and money that was well worth killing for."

"So . . . obviously there's no question of

proving anything at this stage. What you'll do is put the case for honest doubt?"

Charlie nodded.

"That's about it?"

"How will you do it? Write an article?"

"Maybe. I'm a member of the Sneddon Fellowship, courtesy of the West Yorkshire Police. They're going to start a journal."

Oddie raised his eyebrows.

"Good God! You mean you haven't had enough of these literary parasites? If I were you I'd run a mile before I got involved with any literary society."

Charlie chased the last of his potatoes through the steak juices left on his plate.

"Still, they are the audience that would be most interested. And they'd know of my connection with the Suzman case . . ."

"Flap, flap, flap."

"What's that supposed to mean?"

"A late-arriving vulture has caught sight of one last piece of carrion."

The employees of THORNDIKE PRESS hope you have enjoyed this Large Print book. All our Large Print books are designed for easy reading — and they're made to last.

Other Thorndike Large Print books are available at your library, through selected bookstores, or directly from us. Suggestions for books you would like to see in Large Print are always welcome.

For more information about current and upcoming titles, please call or mail your name and address to:

THORNDIKE PRESS
PO Box 159
Thorndike, Maine 04986
800/223-6121
207/948-2962